A STRANGER, A THIEF & A PACK OF LIES

For Meggie and Molly, the real Eenies.

A STRANGER, A THIEF & A PACK OF LIES

MYSTERIES OF ECKERT HOUSE

by CHRIS AUER

2:52
smarter • stronger
deeper • cooler

Zonderkidz

Zonderkidz ®

The children's group of Zondervan

www.zonderkidz.com

A Stranger, A Thief & a Pack of Lies
Copyright © 2004 by Chris Auer

Requests for information should be addressed to:
Zonderkidz, Grand Rapids, Michigan 49530

Library of Congress Cataloging-in-Publication Data
Auer, Chris, 1955-
  A stranger, a thief and a pack of lies / by Chris Auer.
    p. cm.–(2:52 mysteries of Eckert House ; bk. 2)
  Summary: Relying on God's strength, Dan helps solve another mystery at the
Eckert House museum when a man claiming to be Theodore Eckert appears to
pick up his inheritance–a very valuable tapestry that has been missing for years.
  ISBN 0-310-70871-0 (softcover)
  [1. Museums—Fiction. 2. Robbers and outlaws—Fiction. 3. Impersonation—
Fiction. 4. Christian life—Fiction. 5. Mystery and detective stories.] I. Title.
  PZ7.A9113St 2005
  [Fic]--dc22   2004012527

All Scripture quotations, unless otherwise indicated, are taken from the HOLY
BIBLE, NEW INTERNATIONAL VERSION ®. Copyright © 1973, 1978, 1984
by International Bible Society. Used by permission of Zondervan. All Rights
Reserved.

Editor: Amy De Vries
Cover design: Jay Smith–Juicebox Designs
Interior design: Susan Ambs
Art direction: Michelle Lenger and Merit Alderink

Printed in the United States of America

05 06 07 /❖DCI/ 10 9 8 7 6 5 4 3

CONTENTS

AN UNEXPECTED VISITOR

"I don't like being famous."

This was an odd statement, coming from Dan Pruitt.

"Really," he insisted. His two sisters looked at him in disbelief.

Maureen and Eileen were seven and eight, but everyone who saw them thought they were twins. That was partly because they were always

7

together, partly because they looked very much alike, and partly because, when they spoke, they often finished one another's sentences.

"Step back," Maureen ordered.

"Further than usual," Eileen agreed.

Both girls took a giant step away from their brother.

"Cute," said Dan.

In the Pruitt family, when someone made an outrageous statement the others stepped away, pretending that lightning bolts were on their way from heaven.

"Better yet," said Maureen.

"Right," said Eileen.

They turned and ran into the house. The three of them were supposed to be weeding the tomato patch, but his sisters had been doing more teasing than working.

"Mom!" Dan called out. "The Eenies aren't working!" He knew his mother wasn't yet back from taking his grandfather to the doctor's, but he hoped they didn't know.

Dan never called his sisters anything but "The Eenies." Maureen. Eileen. The Eenies just seemed easier. Besides, why address them separately when they were never apart? Whenever he called one, he always got both of them.

The Eenies reappeared at the open kitchen window.

"I don't know about *you*," one of them said in a fake snooty voice, "I *hate* being famous."

"I gave my autograph out *two thousand times* this morning."

"That is so tragic."

"You want to know what's gonna be tragic?" Dan asked. "When you two wake up tomorrow morning with your braids tied together."

"Not if we don't go to sleep!" one of them yelled as they giggled. A minute later Dan heard the front door slam.

Dan had to laugh. He couldn't help it. He thought his sisters were funny. He returned to the rows of tomato plants and started weeding again.

The truth was, Dan really didn't like being famous. He had tried to go to the mall the day before and was surrounded by a crowd wanting his autograph. Because of that, Dan's mother had asked him to stay close to home for a few days. Close to home meant, among other less-than-exciting things, weeding the garden.

There were a couple of reasons why Dan was famous. His first brush with fame was in the middle of the summer when he uncovered a human skeleton on the property of Eckert House. Dan did odd jobs around Eckert House, the former mansion of the wealthiest family in town, which had been turned into a museum. The discovery of the skeleton got him interviewed by local television and newspaper reporters.

Then, a short time later, he was famous all over again when he helped stop an art thief from stealing a valuable statue from the museum. That time, however, it was national reporters who came to Dan's small town of Freemont, Pennsylvania.

Even though Dan was the focus of most of the attention, there was plenty of fame to go around. Dan's cousin Pete and their best friend, Shelby, were a big part of the story, too. The television reports made it all sound like an amusing adventure, but at the time, it was anything but fun.

"You wonder where tomorrow's heroes are?" the reporter had concluded. "Well, they're right here." And with that she had put her arm around Dan's shoulder.

Dan did not feel like a hero. It was his recklessness that had set everything into motion in the first place.

It all ended well, but the story could have had a very different conclusion.

Dan had written and explained everything to his father, a Navy flier who was stationed overseas. He expected a strong letter back, but his father was surprisingly gentle. After expressing his relief that no one was seriously hurt (just a few stitches and some bumps and bruises), he reminded Dan to help his mother as much as possible — especially with the Eenies and his little brother, Jack, who was only four.

Remember, Dan, he concluded, *it's what a man does when no one's looking that really tells him who he is. That's strength.*

The problem was, people were always looking at Dan. He was recognized everywhere he went.

From the front of the house, the Eenies started teasing Dan again.

"Is this where he lives?"

"He is soooo cute."

"Totally."

The sound of their voices indicated that they were standing on the front walk. That gave Dan an idea. He bent down and picked up five very squishy tomatoes that were rotting on the ground. He did some fast calculations, stepped back, and hurled one tomato after another over the roof of the house. One, two, three, four, five — quick as a flash. If luck and skill were with him, there was a good chance that at least one of the tomatoes would hit at least one of the Eenies.

Luck and skill were with him. Seconds later, his sisters' shrieks and squeals told him he had scored a direct hit. Maybe two.

He quickly gathered three more tomatoes. With all of his might he threw them so that they would reach the driveway. Dan figured that was the next logical place for the Eenies to run, and they would consider it out of his range. They were wrong. He had a good arm, and he could reach them where they stood — or rather where they should have been standing.

"Mr. Pruitt!"

The second and third tomatoes had found a target. Unfortunately the target was not the Eenies.

It was Miss Alma Louise Stockton LeMay. Miss Alma, the curator at the museum, was only five feet tall, and she was over seventy years old. Even so, she was the most feared person in all of Freemont. She had a sharp mind and an even sharper tongue.

There was a softer side to Miss Alma, and Dan occasionally got to see it, but he knew that was not going to happen today.

Miss Alma came around the side of the house. She was covered with bits of rotten tomato. She was not happy.

"Miss Alma," Dan cried out with surprise. "I . . . I . . . didn't expect *you* to be out there!"

"No? For whom was this charming surprise intended?" she asked with unusual calm as she dabbed her face with her handkerchief.

"My sisters," Dan answered honestly. "Didn't you see them out there?"

"It's difficult to see anything with tomato oozing in your eyes," she answered.

Dan knew some kind of explosion was coming. "Um, let me get you a towel," he offered as he moved to the house.

"No!" she thundered. "The handkerchief is fine." Dan stopped.

Even dripping with tomato, Miss Alma remained dignified and in control. Within a few minutes she had tidied her face, hair, and shoulders, and informed Dan that his services were needed at Eckert House later that afternoon. She then bid him good-bye.

Dan watched her go, then returned to weeding. He knew that Miss Alma was angry, and he also knew that he would pay the price for it. Ten seconds later, as he bent over to loosen a stubborn weed, SPLAT, an overly ripe tomato hit him right on his backside. It exploded everywhere.

"Yeow! You two are gonna regret that!" he shouted.

"No, Mr. Pruitt," Miss Alma said, "I don't think I will." With that she walked away.

"Miss Alma just pegged me with a tomato," Dan said aloud. He wondered if the stress of the summer had finally gotten to her. "I'm gonna have to keep a close eye on her," he mumbled.

An old shirt and a battered Pittsburgh Pirates baseball cap stuck on a pole in the middle of the vegetable garden served as a scarecrow. Dan pulled down the shirt and used it to get the tomato off the seat of his pants. The shirt and the hat were Grandpa Mike's. So was the vegetable garden. So was the house in which Dan and his family lived.

Grandpa Mike was his mother's father and the reason Dan and his family had moved back to Freemont. When his grandfather had a stroke, he needed someone to take care of him. Dan's Uncle Jeff (his cousin Pete's dad) also lived in Freemont, but Uncle Jeff was having a rough time, and just wasn't up to the task.

By the time Dan had finished wth the garden his mother had returned from the doctor's office, so he went up to Grandpa Mike's room. Dan read to his grandfather every day, first some Scripture, and then the sports page of the newspaper. But Grandpa Mike was so tired from the morning trip to the doctor that he was fast asleep. Dan looked at his grandfather, wondering if he would ever be able to speak again or if he would always have to use a walker to get around.

The day before, Dan had read to his grandfather from Isaiah. *"Those also who are tall in stature will be cut down ... Then a shoot will spring from the stem of Jesse."* It was all about God making sure his people knew who was really in charge, and it was followed by a promise that a Messiah would come and bring his kingdom.

Dan couldn't help but think about how Grandpa Mike was once so tall and strong, and how he was cut down. He knew that the stem of Jesse was a symbol for Jesus, and the "springing up" part made Dan think of the Scripture his father gave him to study before he was shipped out. *"And Jesus grew in*

wisdom and stature, and in favor with God and men."
That word "stature" kept coming up. Dan had looked
it up in the dictionary. In one sense it had to do with
how tall a person was, but to Dan it also meant a
kind of strength. Jesus grew taller and stronger as
he got older. Just like Dan was getting taller. He
wasn't so sure about the stronger part, though.

A glance at the clock told Dan that he wouldn't
have had time to read to his grandfather. Miss Alma
had ordered Dan to be at Eckert House promptly at
two o'clock.

By the time he was ready to leave, he had only
five minutes to get there. Being on time was always
a good idea with Miss Alma. Even though he lived
about three-quarters of a mile away from the
museum, it was mostly downhill, so that wasn't
going to be a problem.

Dan's usual means of transportation around town
was his skateboard. No hill was too steep for him,
and no curve was too dangerous. Although his skateboard had four wheels, the more time he spent on
only two of them, the happier he was.

He was making good time when he hit the long,
steep slope down Filkins Street. Eckert House was
just at the bottom of the hill. Dan would have been

on time, a minute early, in fact, but he happened to see Uncle Jeff coming out of his house. Uncle Jeff was wearing a security guard's uniform.

Dan leaned back on his skateboard with all of his weight, tilted to the left, made a tight circle, and jumped off the board. As he did, he flicked it with his foot so that it flew up in the air. He caught it neatly and ended up just a couple of feet in front of his uncle.

"Hey, Uncle Jeff, what's with the uniform?" Dan asked.

Uncle Jeff had jerked back when Dan stopped so abruptly in front of him. Dan sometimes forgot how alarming the stunts he pulled on his skateboard were to other people. Uncle Jeff raised a shaky hand to his head.

"Um . . . hey, Dan," he managed to say. "Next time give me a little warning, okay?"

"New job?" Dan asked hopefully.

It had been quite a few months since his uncle had been employed, and it was something his cousin Pete worried about. Uncle Jeff had a hard time keeping a job when he drank, but then when he stopped drinking last year, he couldn't get a job. It was very hard on the whole family.

"Yeah, as a matter of fact, you'll be seeing a lot of me." Dan's uncle went on to explain that he had been hired as part of the extra security that Eckert House now needed. Dan's previous exploits involved a piece of art that the museum had owned for years, which to everyone's surprise, turned out to be quite valuable. Now hundreds of people wanted to see it.

"Guess I owe you a big thank you," Uncle Jeff concluded. "That little statue you found requires round-the-clock attention." Then with a wink he added, "I'm one of the baby-sitters."

They continued their conversation as they walked down the hill toward the mansion. There was a small part of Dan that was worried. What if his uncle started drinking again? What if he didn't show up one day? What if something happened while he was on duty and he couldn't handle it?

Dan was happy for Uncle Jeff, but considering his uncle's past, he couldn't help but wonder why Miss Alma had hired him. For the second time that day, he started to worry about Miss Alma. She suddenly had a lot of responsibility for someone her age, and she was not the kind of person who would ask for help—even if she needed it.

Dan's conversation with his uncle caused him to be five minutes late. They entered through the employees' entrance at the back of the house, a door that opened directly into the kitchen. Miss Alma was there waiting. She had changed her clothes.

"Well, Mr. Pruitt," she said, "your aim may be accurate, but your timeliness leaves much to be desired." As she said this, she reached out, took off Dan's baseball cap, and handed it to him.

"Yes, Miss Alma," he replied. There really wasn't anything else he could say.

"Mr. March," she said, nodding to Dan's uncle.

"Miss Alma." Uncle Jeff nodded. He had remembered to remove his hat. Not only that, but Dan noticed that his hair was neatly cut, his shoes were shined, and his uniform was crisply ironed.

"I hope you don't mind me coming early," he said. "My shift doesn't start until three, but I wanted to get better acquainted with the place."

"An excellent idea," she replied. Miss Alma shot Dan a look clearly implying that coming to work early was something *he* might want to consider as well.

"Want me to show him around?" Dan asked, hoping to get away from Miss Alma.

"No," was the swift reply. "Rick is waiting for you out back."

Rick was Rick Doheny, the official caretaker of Eckert House. He had recently returned after an absence of almost two months. When Dan first started working at the museum, Rick was out with a dislocated shoulder, and (so Dan believed) Miss Alma needed a certain amount of people to boss around or she wasn't happy. Rick was a nice enough guy. He had wanted to play professional baseball, but was injured in college. He was the son of Mrs. Doheny, the timid little woman who sat behind a desk in the front hall and greeted visitors when they entered.

"Feel free to join him at any time, Mr. Pruitt. I know you've had a stressful day, so if you'd rather wait in here, put up your feet, and have a cool drink, then by all means, please do."

Uncle Jeff covered his laughter by pretending to cough, then left with Miss Alma. Dan stood in the middle of the kitchen for a moment. He had just received sharp words from Miss Alma, but he found that he was smiling. Even as he wondered why, it hit him. Life was approaching normal again.

Yes, his father was still overseas and still in danger, but every day he was gone was a day sooner that he would return. True, Grandpa Mike still struggled with the results of his stroke, but just today the doctor said he thought there was some improvement. Uncle Jeff hadn't had a drink in a year, and now he had a job, so things were looking up there, too.

Normal. Maybe it was time to stop worrying so much and start enjoying himself.

The back door opened. Dan expected to see Rick and was just about to apologize for being late. But it wasn't Rick. It was a little man about Miss Alma's age. He was dressed in an elegant summer suit, carried a cane, and wore an equally elegant straw hat. He was smiling broadly, and he looked so pleasant that Dan couldn't help but smile back.

"May I help you?" Dan offered.

"I don't know," the man answered. "What did you have in mind?"

This wasn't exactly what Dan expected to hear. "May I take you around front? Visitors are supposed to use that door," he finally said.

"As well they should," the little man replied. "But I'm not a visitor. My name is Theodore Eckert, and this is my house."

An Unexpected Discovery

"And then Miss Alma said, 'How very nice to meet you.' Just like that. Not 'Get out of this house before I throw you out.' Not a threat to call the police. She was all smiles and 'Let me show you around.' It was unbelievable!"

Dan plucked a leaf from a branch of the tree in which he was sitting, crumpled it, and threw it to the ground. He had just finished telling Pete and

Shelby about Theodore Eckert and how Miss Alma accepted it all so calmly. The three of them were sitting in a tree behind Pete's house, a spot where they went to discuss anything that bothered them.

"I tell you, I think she's slipping," Dan added.

Shelby and Pete agreed.

"We'll just have to keep an eye on her," Shelby decided. "If Miss Alma isn't suspicious of someone walking into Eckert House like that, then something's wrong."

Dan was glad Pete and Shelby saw the situation the same way he did.

"Look," he said, "the last thing I want is anything that even comes close to another adventure. But I don't believe this Eckert guy is real for a second. We have to figure out who he really is. Agreed?"

They did. As usual, Pete looked for something positive to say.

"And when we do, we'll all get on the news again."

Dan groaned. "No publicity."

Shelby laughed. "Speak for yourself. It's been over a week since my last interview. I think the world needs to see more of me."

"Well, this time around we better take notes and make sure we keep the facts straight," Dan said.

The last time Dan and Shelby ran to the police to say that Pete had been kidnapped, they had been treated like a couple of crazy kids, which, in all fairness, is what they sounded like. Because of that, Dan knew that if he was ever going to report anything out of the ordinary again, he better have the facts to back it up.

"Notes!" Pete cried. "You guys are not gonna believe this!" He swung down out of the tree and ran into the house.

"What do you suppose that was that all about?" asked Shelby.

"Don't know. C'mon, let's see what's going on."

Minutes later, Dan and Shelby stood in Pete's dining room. On the table in front of them was the World War II diary Miss Alma had given Dan. It was written by a boy whose father had gone away to fight in Europe. Miss Alma had presented it to Dan as something of a challenge. She wanted him to see if he could find out who wrote it, and how it had ended up in the library at Eckert House.

Dan took her up on the challenge, but he suspected Miss Alma had really given it to him because of the similarity of his situation and the boy in the diary. Both boys had fathers in the military that were overseas fighting, and both of them (although Dan never said it out loud) wondered if their dads would ever come back.

The diary had been given to Dan, but both Pete and Shelby had borrowed it to search for clues. Pete had been studying it for the past few days.

"Look, there at the bottom of the entry for January 21, 1943," Pete said, pointing to some faint marks made in pencil.

The rest of the diary had been written with a fountain pen in watery blue ink. It was a page Dan had certainly seen before, but the pencil marks were so light, he had not paid close attention to them. He had been more interested in the words of the diary than what was scribbled in the margins.

"It looks like . . . music notes?" Dan said, squinting. There wasn't much about music that interested him.

"Exactly," Pete exclaimed. He pointed to the five thin lines and explained that they made up the staff, and that the 2 over the 4 was something called the time signature. The tiny dots on the lines were the notes. He then picked up his trumpet. "I think this is what it's supposed to sound like." He raised the instrument to his lips and blew. The six loud bleats that exploded out of the horn sounded like an animal being poked with a stick. "What do you think?" Pete asked excitedly.

"I think that every moose within a hundred miles is gonna show up at your front door," Dan answered.

"Exactly," Pete said again.

"Um, Pete," Shelby said, showing more patience than Dan, "you obviously think this means something, but what?"

"That isn't music," Dan grunted.

"Exactly," Pete shouted.

"Stop saying that," Dan yelled back.

It took Dan and Shelby awhile, but they eventually got Pete to explain what he was getting at; mainly that these notes weren't *supposed* to be music, that he thought they were a possible clue to the identity of the diary's author. The notes were the E and the C above middle C.

"They could be his initials, but I think they're something else."

"Why?" Dan asked.

"Because it's all too clever to be that simple," Pete answered. He pointed to the numbers. "Let's start here. The two and the four could be twenty-four, or you could add them and they could be six, or even forty-two, I suppose. Or," and here Pete paused for dramatic effect, "it could be two *times* four, which is eight."

Shelby thought Pete was on to something. "*You* think it means 'eight.' Why?"

"Because, like I said, numbers at the beginning of music like that are called a time signature. Two *times* four."

Dan kept quiet. It made sense. It was the kind of code he might use if he were trying to keep his identity a secret. If he were writing a diary like this, a record of his deepest feelings and fears, he would definitely not want anyone to know he was writing it.

"Eight . . . eight . . . But eight what?" he wondered.

"Well, the E, the first note there, could be the first letter of his first name, but then I got to thinking what else an E could stand for . . ." Pete let his voice trail off.

"How about east?" Dan finally said.

"Of course," Shelby added.

Pete smiled and nodded. "I was hoping that's what you'd say."

"Wait. Did you say that it's the E above middle C?" Dan asked.

"Yeah."

The three friends stared at the page for a moment. Pete held his breath. Then, at almost the exact same time, Dan and Shelby shouted together.

"Middle Street."

"Exactly," Pete added. Middle Street was just north of the intersection in Freemont known as the Four Corners.

"What are the streets above Middle Street?"

Middle Street ran east to west, and they named the streets north of Middle, or *above* it, as they would appear on a map. Nelson, Miles, Dewey, and . . .

"East Crane." Dan and Shelby shouted in unison.

"E and C above middle C," Shelby added. "The next two notes are E and then C again. *East Crane.*"

Dan was the first one out the door.

To get to East Crane Street, they had to go up Filkins, take a left on Church Street (which ran north and south), and continue through the Four Corners. The first street beyond the intersection was Nelson, then Miles, then Dewey, and finally East Crane. They didn't slow down, and they were completely out of breath when they turned right onto East Crane.

"Number eight," said Shelby, panting.

The town of Freemont was built along the eastern side of the Morgan River. It was flat right near the river itself, but to the east, the town climbed a series of hills. East Crane ran up the steepest of these hills, and number eight had to be near the top.

"Number twelve," Shelby said, pointing to a solid red brick house that had been built in the 1920s. This part of Freemont was developed around that time, a time when everyone seemed to have money, so the lawns were deep and wide, the trees planted so long ago were now tall and stately, and the homes were large and elegant.

Number ten was also brick. The hedge that separated it from number eight had grown quite high over the years, so the house on the other side, the house they were looking for, was hidden from view as they approached. Dan was not prepared for what he saw when he cleared the hedge.

"That doesn't make sense," Dan said.

The three of them stood looking at a small yellow house that didn't seem to fit in this neighborhood at all. It didn't fit because it was fairly new, looking as if it had been built within the past few years. The number on the house was clearly marked. "Eight" was over the door in shiny brass letters.

"Well, there it is. Eight East Crane," Shelby said.

"This house was not here in 1943."

The three of them stood there in silence.

"Now what?" Pete asked, trying hard not to show his disappointment.

"Now nothing," Shelby offered. "We were wrong." She turned to go. Pete followed.

Dan did not move. Dan was having one of those moments; one of those intense don't-talk-to-me-I'm-thinking-and-it-could-be-big moments. Shelby and Pete waited.

"Look at those trees," Dan said, pointing to four very large, very old maple trees that were about one hundred feet apart and formed what looked like a perfect square around the house.

"We're looking," Shelby said.

"Now look across the street. And next door, and at the house next to that."

Pete and Shelby did. There were other maple trees, each about the same size as the ones around the little yellow house. Like those trees, they, too were placed at the four corners of each of the larger homes.

"What's the same and what's different?" Dan asked, obviously knowing the answer. Neither Shelby nor Pete could tell him. "What's the *same*," Dan explained, "is that the trees around the yellow house were planted at about the same distance as the trees around the bigger houses. And from their size, it looks like they were all planted at about the same time. What's different—"

"Is the house," Shelby cried. "There used to be a bigger house where the yellow one now stands!"

"Exactly," Dan shouted.

Once again, Dan took the lead. He walked right up to the front door of number eight East Crane Street and rang the bell.

"Go away," they heard a faint voice shout from inside the house. "Whatever it is you're selling, I don't want it."

"We're not selling anything. We just have a couple of questions to ask you."

Repeated ringing of the bell (not to mention quite a few knocks) didn't bring anyone to the door. They had a whispered discussion about what they should do, decided there wasn't anything they really could do, and headed back down the front walk.

"That's that," Pete said with a shrug.

"That's what you think," said Dan, and he marched to the house directly across the street.

Dan had discovered that summer that he was the kind of person that people just seemed to like. He also discovered, after about his ten thousandth television interview, that he could turn on the charm when he needed it—which is precisely what he did with Mrs. Sorge, who lived at number nine East Crane Street. Mrs. Sorge knew who Dan was and was more than eager to answer his questions.

"Why, that's Will Stoller's house," she offered. "He lives there all alone and doesn't answer his door to anyone. Not even to the neighbors."

Mrs. Sorge went on to explain that ladies from local churches dropped off groceries and such, and that occasionally a doctor came and went, but that, to her knowledge, he never so much as set a foot outside the house.

Dan steered the conversation around to the house itself, and asked why it was so different from all the others in the neighborhood.

"Well, it's only ten years old or so. The old one caught fire. Of course it was out of the question that an old man like Will Stoller would rebuild it as big as it once was. No, he built what he needed, no more, no less."

"How long did he live in the original house?" Dan asked, trying not to sound too nosey.

"His whole life," was the answer. She believed Will Stoller had been born there in the '20s or '30s.

"Then he might have been twelve in 1943!" Pete said with more than a little excitement. The author of the diary had been twelve when he wrote it.

"Yes, I suppose he might have been," Mrs. Sorge answered, now a little suspicious. "Why are you asking all these questions about Mr. Stoller?"

Dan explained about the diary. "Do you know whether his father fought in World War II?" he asked.

Mrs. Sorge did not know. "One thing's for sure," she said just before she went inside. "You won't find anything out by talking to Will Stoller. That man won't let anyone near him that he doesn't already know." She wished them all a good day and went back to her baking. They walked home in silence. They were all discouraged.

"Thanks, Pete," Dan said, only half kidding. "Now we have two mysteries to solve—Will Stoller and Theodore Eckert."

An Unexpected Story

Rick Doheny was an emotional guy. The first time Dan met Rick, he gave Dan a bear hug and thanked him for keeping the grass so neat and trim while he was gone.

"Look at that lawn, dude," Rick had said. Many of the sentences Rick spoke ended in "dude." It was something that took a little getting used to. "You've kept it so green, dude. Only a dude who really loved grass could take care of it like that. You're the best, dude." Rick then burst into tears. Apparently he really liked a green lawn.

The day after Dan, Pete, and Shelby had been so disappointed about hitting a dead end with the diary, Dan came to work and found Rick in the kitchen crying. He was reading the sports page.

"Rick, are you okay?"

"Hey, dude," Rick said, wiping his eyes. He wasn't the least bit embarrassed that Dan had found him crying. "Look, dude, the Boston Red Sox are in first place. It's a beautiful thing, dude." Apparently the Boston Red Sox affected Rick in much the same way that a really green lawn did. And little puppies. And the movie *Deadly Fists of Deadly Death*. Dan had seen Rick weep over all of these.

"Yes, it is," Dan answered. "The Red Sox are ... are ... beautiful. Dude." Every now and then Dan tried calling Rick "dude" as well. Rick seemed to like that. Dan didn't think he was as good at it as Rick.

Miss Alma came into the kitchen. She was holding a stack of bills.

"Rick, you're driving me crazy," she said. Miss Alma saw Dan. "Good morning, Mr. Pruitt."

"Morning, Miss Alma."

She made a point of looking at the clock. Dan was on time, but she didn't acknowledge it.

Miss Alma continued with Rick. One of Rick's responsibilities at Eckert House was to keep the two white vans gassed up and running smoothly. He was issued a credit card to take care of those expenses, and it was about those bills that Miss Alma was complaining.

"Look at these credit card bills. Why can't you just fill the vans with gas all at once rather than every time you go out? You've been doing this for years; I can't take it anymore. Like this: $12.56 at the Gas 'n' Go, and then $20.16 at Fuel Town. On the same day!"

Rick had a logical explanation for this. At least it was logical to Rick.

"Well, you see, Miss A, this is the way it was ..." Miss Alma was spared Rick calling her "dude," but he replaced it with "Miss A." "I was pumping the gas, you know, minding my own business, when I look across the street and what do I see? I see that the same gas is selling at Fuel Town for an entire penny cheaper than what I'm paying at Gas 'n' Go. Now does that seem right to you? Of course not. So what do I do? I just stopped pumping that second. I drove myself across the street and spent your money where it would go further. I'm just sorry that Gas 'n' Go got the twelve dollars and fifty-six cents in the first place."

Miss Alma took off her glasses and rubbed the bridge of her nose. Dan knew this was not a good sign. It meant that she was very, very irritated. She replaced her glasses and showed Rick the bill again.

"Yes, but the very next day you spent $14.50 at Fuel Town, and then you went immediately across the street and spent $12 at Gas 'n' Go! Why?"

Rick was either missing Miss Alma's growing anger, or he had decided to ignore it.

"Okay, now here's what happened with that. I had the other van 'cause it needed gas, too. Well, I wasn't gonna make the same mistake twice, so I went right to Fuel Town. I didn't even so much as *look* across the street — and my buddy, Glen, was working there that morning. I mean, c'mon, when you're charging a whole penny more per gallon for gas, I think we can forget about being polite, right?

"Then before I started pumping, I bought a few cases of motor oil. They were having a great sale. I know you might think I bought too much, but when it comes to saving money, I always say — "

"Please, Rick, as fascinating as this is, I don't want all these details. The next thing I know, you'll be telling me what you had for breakfast that day."

"An egg burrito. From Taco Tim's. Two, as a matter of fact, 'cause it was a two-for-one deal, *and* your beverage was free. Also, if you—"

"Rick!" Miss Alma had finally snapped.

Rick's chin started to quiver. His eyes were moist. "Um, so anyway," he continued with some difficulty, ". . . I, um . . . I buy the oil (sniff) and I start pumping gas, and then I . . . um . . . look across the street to Gas 'n' Go, and . . . and now *their* gas is a penny cheaper than the gas I'm pumping at Fuel Town." Rick turned away and blew his nose. "Excuse me."

Miss Alma never quite knew how to handle Rick when he got this way. She finally just handed him her handkerchief. "I see," she finally said. "So all this is your attempt to save Eckert House some money."

"Yes," Rick blurted out.

Dan got a quick glimpse of the credit card bill. The list was much longer than the four charges that Miss Alma had shared, and they all seemed to be from different gas stations. He couldn't help but smile. Rick was definitely a character.

Miss Alma opened her mouth as if she was going to say something, but changed her mind. Dan knew that any further questions would only end up with more and more complicated answers from Rick, and that they'd most likely end up knowing not only what he had for breakfast each day, but lunch and dinner, too.

"Thank you," Miss Alma finally said.

"You know, Miss A, with you-know-who poking around here, isn't it good that I'm saving you money? I mean—"

"Yes, Rick. Thank you." Miss Alma left.

Dan waited for Rick to pull himself together and then asked him what he meant about it being good that he was saving Eckert House money. Dan was shocked by the answer. If Theodore Eckert turned out to be a real Eckert, Rick explained, then every penny that was spent by and for Eckert House would have to be approved by him. In fact there was a good chance the museum would be closed, and he would live there as so many of the Eckerts had in the past.

"Is it that serious?" asked Dan.

Rick could only nod. "I think I'm history, dude. I don't think that Eckert guy likes me."

"Oh, c'mon," Dan said, trying to be cheerful. "Everybody likes you. Dude."

"Not him."

"Why do you say that? Give me one good reason. I bet you can't," Dan challenged.

"Well," said Rick, thinking, "maybe you're right."

"I know I am," Dan assured him.

"Of course the other day he did come up to me and say, 'Rick, I don't like you.' What do you think he meant by that?"

Rick and Dan spent the rest of the morning cutting the large lawn. As they worked, Rick grew calmer. This was because, as Rick put it, once he was concentrating on his beloved lawn, he "was in the zone, dude."

Dan wasn't concentrating on the lawn. He was focused on Miss Alma and Theodore Eckert, who had appeared shortly after Dan and Rick started cutting. Miss Alma and Theodore Eckert inspected the outside of the house. Then they moved inside, where Dan caught glimpses of them going from room to room.

Dan imagined that the old gentleman was quietly adding up the worth of everything in the house. Why was Miss Alma going along with it? Dan knew that one way or another, he had to speak to Miss Alma before he went home. All he needed was an excuse, a reason that could get her talking, but nothing he could think of seemed reasonable.

When they were done, Rick stood with Dan beneath one of the largest trees at the corner of the house and nodded. He was pleased.

"Dude, this is what life's all about," he said. "The sweet smell of cut grass, the fruit of our labors, the shade of a tree." Rick looked up. "Those old dudes really knew what they were doing when they planted trees near the corners of their houses."

Dan didn't understand what Rick meant. Rick explained that the shade of the trees kept the houses cool in the heat, but because they lost their leaves when the weather turned cold, they allowed sunshine in to help warm the houses in the winter.

"That's it!" Dan exclaimed. He excused himself and went inside to look for Miss Alma.

Miss Alma was in her tiny office on the third floor. She was still talking to Theodore Eckert. As Dan walked toward the open door, he tried to hear what they were saying without technically eavesdropping. He did this by walking slowly and quietly.

"Well, Miss Alma, I certainly hope that satisfies you. I'll be back tomorrow." Theodore Eckert's voice was soft and had a trace of an accent. It wasn't Southern or

Midwestern, but it was *something*. Dan couldn't quite put his finger on it.

The elderly gentlemen came out of the office and nodded politely to Dan. Dan had only seen Theodore Eckert a few times since his arrival, and every time he wore a three-piece suit, a bow tie, and a hat (which he never failed to take off once he was inside). He also always wore gloves. Dan thought this was just part of the overall elegant outfit, but as Theodore reached the top of the stairs he took one glove off to adjust a button. His exposed left hand was red and swollen. He saw Dan looking at him.

"Eczema," he said. "It's a skin disease. Most uncomfortable." Once the glove was back on his hand, he smiled at Dan, headed down the main staircase and out the front door.

"Are you going to stand out there all day, Mr. Pruitt?" Miss Alma asked when Dan did not move.

Rick's comments about the trees had given Dan the idea to bring Miss Alma up-to-date with the diary: how they thought they broke the code, and how they found Will Stoller but were unable to speak with him. She listened very carefully to the whole story.

"Will Stoller," she finally said. "Now there's a name from the past . . ."

"You know him," Dan shouted.

"Mr. Pruitt, please," she scolded.

"You do."

"I know many people. And yes, he's one of the many I know," she replied.

"Do you think he could be the one who wrote the diary?"

"Possibly."

"So what would you suggest we do next?" he asked.

"Find out, of course." Miss Alma fell silent. It was awhile before she spoke again. Dan sat very still, waiting. "Mr. Pruitt, why don't you ask me what you really came in here to ask."

Dan knew Miss Alma well enough not to try and pretend. He blurted it out. "Miss Alma, this guy, Theodore Eckert, we don't know anything about him, and yet you seem to think he's telling the truth. How can you let him come in here and maybe take away everything you've worked so hard for? I don't understand any of it."

Miss Alma was unusually calm, something that surprised Dan, considering how emotional he'd just been.

"First of all, nothing within these walls or on this property is mine. I simply take care of it. Second, since the museum became somewhat famous, Theodore Eckert is the first person to walk in and claim it all, but he may not be the last. And third, he has shown me some very interesting proof that he is who he says he is."

Without Dan even asking, Miss Alma pulled out an envelope and removed some papers and photographs. Her explanation was brief.

Hollis Eckert was a familiar name. This was a man who had threatened to accuse an innocent boy of murder just to protect the Eckert name and keep his niece from getting married.

"Hollis Eckert was not a nice man," Miss Alma said without going any further, but the way she said it made Dan feel that there was a lot more she could say if she chose to. She took a deep breath. "Theodore Eckert claims that Hollis Eckert was his father."

That's where the papers and the photographs came in. A birth certificate, old passports, school records, citizenship papers: it was quite a collection. According to Theodore, Hollis had a separate family in Europe before World War II. Records kept by the

Eckert family, and checked by Miss Alma herself, confirmed that Hollis Eckert did indeed make many trips overseas between World War I and World War II, especially to a town in Belgium where Theodore claimed he was born. Theodore's mother was an American from California with no family ties, who supported herself as an artist. She met Hollis and married him, never knowing until many years later that he already had a wife and children in America. When the Nazis invaded Belgium, Theodore and his mother were separated and never saw each other again.

45

"If he knew who his father was, why didn't he come over here after the war?" Dan wanted to know.

"He did. He says he spent the summer of 1951 here in this house. With Hollis Eckert." Dan couldn't believe what he was hearing. Miss Alma continued. The story, like everything else connected to Theodore Eckert, was full of just enough facts that it could be true.

During the summer of 1951, the Eckert family took a trip to the Grand Canyon. Hollis Eckert stayed behind. Theodore claimed he knocked on the door, introduced himself to Hollis, showed him the very papers that were now on Miss Alma's desk, and convinced him that he was his son.

Before the family returned, Hollis gave Theodore a small sum of money as well as a promise. There was a secret treasure within Eckert House that was meant just for Theodore, a treasure that he was free to claim any time after the death of Hollis Eckert.

Dan couldn't stay quiet any longer. "And now he's here to claim the whole house because we have a priceless statue and a lot of other neat stuff which the whole world knows about, thanks to me. He figures he can have it all!"

Miss Alma was still calm. "We're going to take this one step at a time. We don't know what's going to happen yet."

Dan picked up the documents and the photographs. Most were yellow with age, some were written in French, others in German. None were in English. It was the photographs that interested him more. One was taken in Paris in the 1960s. Theodore Eckert was standing next to a woman who looked to be about his age.

"This woman looks familiar," Dan said.

"She should," Miss Alma answered. "You've seen many pictures of her. That's Ethel Eckert. That photograph, more than anything, is what makes me think this man may be telling the truth."

Miss Alma explained that she and Ethel kept in touch over the years until Ethel passed away. Ethel *had* visited Paris around the time the picture was taken.

"Very few people would know that. This photo speaks for itself."

Dan decided it was time to make one last argument.

"Miss Alma, all of this stuff . . . these papers, these photographs . . . we don't know if any of it's real and you're acting like it all is! Do you realize how easy it would be for all of this stuff to be faked? Please don't let this guy do this to us. He's a crook. I just know he is! Did you ever just know something deep, deep inside? You gotta trust me on this!"

Miss Alma didn't turn around. "It's been a long time since I was that sure of anything, Mr. Pruitt." She let out a sigh. "However, Theodore has promised me that tomorrow I'll believe he's the son of Hollis Eckert. He's going to show me the treasure that he says was hidden in this house just for him."

"But, Miss Alma—"

"Why don't you join us at ten o'clock and see just what it is he's going to do."

AN UNEXPECTED TREASURE

The first thing Dan always did when he got home was to check and see if there was a letter from his dad. If there wasn't — and there wasn't that afternoon — he ran to the computer to see if there was an email from him. There were no emails either.

"Hey, Mom," he called out, "have you heard from Dad today?"

"No, honey," she yelled back. "Dinner's in a few minutes."

Dan frowned and chewed his bottom lip. He hadn't heard from his father in almost a week.

"Okay, I'm *not* worried," he said aloud. That helped. A little. So did the Bible verse his father gave him before he left. *"And Jesus grew in wisdom and stature, and in favor with God and men."* Dan repeated it several times, looking at himself in the mirror as he did. Once again, for some strange reason, the word "stature" jumped out at him. He stood on his toes to see what he'd look like an inch or so taller.

"Stature . . . strength," he murmured. Behind him he heard two familiar giggles.

"He spends a lot of time looking at himself in the mirror, doesn't he?"

"I guess he likes what he sees."

"I'm glad somebody does."

Dan decided to ignore them. He had something much more important to talk to the Eenies about. He needed their help.

"Here's the deal," he explained. "I'll pay you two dollars if you'll do the dishes for me tonight."

The Eenies looked at each other. They didn't even need to think about it.

"Three dollars."

"Each."

"Each!" Dan was outraged.

"Take it . . ."

". . . or leave it."

Dan wasn't in a position to argue. He took it. As soon as dinner was over he left for Shelby's house six dollars poorer.

Shelby sat at her computer staring at the two photographs Dan had placed in front of her.

"Can you do it?" he asked.

"We'll never know unless I try," she answered.

"That's the spirit."

They worked until almost nine o'clock that night. Dan went home very happy with what she had done. On his way, he swung by number eight East Crane, the home of Will Stoller. The dark night made him almost invisible, and he stood next to a large tree near the sidewalk and stared at the house. There were no lights on inside. The only sounds were the crickets and the occasional bark of a dog far down the steep hill.

This was a very peaceful part of town. It was still August, but the nights were already cooler; autumn was on the way. Once school started, Dan knew that he wouldn't have time to look for the person who wrote the diary. Maybe because it had been awhile since he'd heard from his father, it suddenly seemed more urgent to find out. The longer it was between letters, the more important the diary felt. There was someone else in the world that knew exactly how Dan felt, and he'd gotten through it. If that person was still alive, Dan wanted to talk to him.

"How do I get to you, Mr. Stoller?" he whispered.

Suddenly Dan froze. He realized that he was being watched—from inside the house. There was a shadowy figure in the front window. Dan didn't know what to do, so he did nothing. He was fairly sure he couldn't be seen, so he stood very still. After a few minutes, the figure melted back into the darkness. Dan breathed a sigh of relief and turned toward home.

The next morning, Dan knocked on Pete's door before heading down to Eckert House.

"Is your dad in?" Dan asked. He figured that he would go to the museum with Uncle Jeff. He hadn't discussed Theodore Eckert with his uncle, but he was pretty sure Uncle Jeff didn't trust the newcomer either. Pete seemed nervous when he stepped out onto the porch.

"Um . . . Dad's not feeling so well today. I think he's going to call in sick."

Dan frowned. In the past, this was how Pete acted when his father got drunk and couldn't get out of bed. "Do you need any help?" he asked.

"He really is sick, Dan. I promise. He has the flu or something."

Now Dan was stuck. The thing about Pete was, he never lied. Still, there was the strong possibility that Pete had only convinced himself that his father was sick.

"Well," Dan finally said, "if you need me for anything, I'm around."

"Thanks." Then, to change the subject, Pete asked what Dan had in the large envelope he was carrying.

"Something Shelby and I worked on last night. I'll show you later. I've got to run." He hopped back on his skateboard and headed down the steep hill.

When he got to Eckert House, Dan went up to the third floor and placed the envelope on Miss Alma's desk. He wrote "Confidential" on it, and then walked down to the front hall to wait.

Dan was all alone in the big hall as the clock struck ten. The museum was closed for the morning. Dan walked around Loretta, his nickname for the statue of the little angel that had stood for years out in the back of the house and now was in a place of honor in the center of the front hall. She was all cleaned up, of course, and he had to admit she looked pretty good.

"Well, are you proud of yourself?" he asked as he patted her foot. "You got us into this mess."

A minute later, Miss Alma came down the stairs with Theodore Eckert and Mrs. Doheny. Dan's Mom was as emotional as her son—just emotional about different things. One of those things was Dan. She considered Dan nothing less than a hero, and she always gave him a big, squishy hug whenever she saw him.

"There's my brave boy!" she exclaimed. "Did you get the cookies I sent over?"

"Yes, ma'am. Thank you very much."

"And the cake?"

"It was great."

"What about the peach pie?"

"Even better than the cake."

Miss Alma cut in. "Are you trying to reward the boy or kill him with sugar?"

Much to Dan's surprise, Theodore Eckert spoke directly to him.

"Miss Alma says you're to help us with any heavy lifting that needs to be done this morning."

Dan looked to Miss Alma for confirmation. She nodded. "I'm here for whatever needs to be done," he said. Miss Alma may very well have wanted him along for "heavy lifting" as Theodore Eckert put it, but Dan suspected there was more to it than that. Exactly what he didn't know, but he trusted Miss Alma. She had something else in mind.

"Look sharp, Mr. Pruitt," she ordered, and then Dan knew. She wanted him to be an extra pair of eyes, to watch everything very carefully.

Theodore walked into the Main Salon. It was the largest room in Eckert House. At the far end was an enormous fireplace — a grown man could actually stand up inside it. It was framed in marble. In the white stone, scenes from the Old Testament were carved: Abraham and Isaac, the parting of the Red Sea, Moses receiving the Ten Commandments, the Israelites crossing the Jordan into the Promised Land, King Solomon's Temple. It was beautiful.

Theodore marched right over to the fireplace, and just the way he did it made Dan's heart beat faster. Dan knew that there was a secret door on the far side of the fireplace, a door that opened onto a hidden staircase that wound around the main chimney to the upper floors of the mansion. He had been trapped inside the passageway once and managed to get out at the fireplace. However, he had no idea how to open the secret door from the outside to get in.

"Isn't it a grand piece of architecture?" Theodore exclaimed as he examined the carvings. Just the way he said it, Dan knew that he knew. He didn't know how, but this man was very familiar with Eckert House. He wasn't pretending.

His gloved hand brushed across the carving of the Hebrews escaping Pharaoh's army through the parted waters. He touched a particular spot, and there was a loud click from the far side of the fireplace. A thin door concealed in the paneling sprung open. Mrs. Doheny gasped, but neither Dan nor Miss Alma reacted. Dan and Miss Alma had never actually spoken about the secret passageway, but from her lack of surprise, Dan realized that she must know all about it.

"One moment, please," Theodore said as he stepped through the door. A few seconds later he appeared, holding an old envelope. He closed the door behind him. "My father left this here for me in case there should be any questions." He handed the envelope to Miss Alma. "Would you like to read what it says? I already know. I was there when he wrote it, sealed it in this envelope, and placed it inside that door. That was in August of 1951."

Miss Alma took the envelope and opened it. She scanned the contents and then read aloud: "If anyone doubts that Theodore Eckert is my son, let The Kellenberg Prodigal prove him wrong."

"The Kellenberg Prodigal? What's that?" asked Dan.

Miss Alma explained it was a valuable fifteenth century tapestry that the Eckerts once owned. It hadn't been seen in more than fifty years. It was assumed that someone had sold it when the Eckert fortunes started to dry up, but it had never appeared in a museum or even in someone's private collection for that matter. It had simply vanished.

Dan knew that a tapestry was a picture woven into fabric. He wanted to ask what it was worth, but decided against it. Mrs. Doheny's gasp at the mention of its name told him that it was worth a lot.

"Now that I've established that it was indeed given to me, let me show you where it is," Theodore said as he strode briskly from the room. They all followed him.

Once on the second floor, he proceeded down the hall, counting as he went along. When he reached seven, he stopped.

"Right here," he said, pointing to one of the mahogany panels that covered the lower half of the wall. He knocked on it. He then knocked on the one before it. "Hear the difference?" he asked. They did. The second panel was solid wood, but the panel he was interested in sounded hollow. He then took out a pocketknife and began prying a piece of molding away from the wall.

"Miss Alma, are you sure he should be doing this?" Mrs. Doheny cried out, alarmed.

"It's fine," Miss Alma replied.

Removing the small piece of molding revealed a little hook-like device underneath. No one said a word as Theodore pulled it. The hollow panel below it slid open. Theodore stepped aside.

"Unless I'm mistaken — and I don't believe I am — you'll find what we're looking for just inside."

"Mr. Pruitt, I believe this is where you come in," Miss Alma said.

Theodore handed Dan a small flashlight, and Dan got on his hands and knees to crawl into the dark hole. He looked over his shoulder before he disappeared.

"If I don't make it, give Rick my baseball cards," Dan said to Mrs. Doheny, trying to lighten the mood.

"Merciful heavens!" Mrs. Doheny exclaimed, tears instantly forming in her eyes.

"Oh, for pity's sake, he's joking," Miss Alma snapped.

The space through which Dan was crawling was about three feet wide. Dan had an excellent sense of direction, and he realized that he must be quite close to the secret stairway.

"Is it there? Did you find it?" Theodore called in to him. For the first time he sounded anxious instead of in control. Dan wanted very much for the answer to that question to be no, but even as he thought this, the beam of the flashlight swept across a cylindrical object about five feet long. It was wrapped in brown paper.

"There's something here!" he hollered.

"Wonderful," Theodore shouted. "Bring it out!"

Dan hoped the object was nothing more than an old, worthless rug or a large piece of canvas used to cover furniture, but deep inside he knew exactly what it was that he was dragging out. And he knew that because of it, Theodore Eckert's claims were going to be very difficult to disprove.

Several minutes later the tapestry was unwrapped and unrolled right there in the hall. Miss Alma's reaction told Dan everything he needed to know: it was The Kellenberg Prodigal. The scene depicted was the Return of the Prodigal Son from the gospel of Luke. It showed the wayward son embraced by his tearful father, who looked to heaven in thanksgiving. Other members of the household were gathered around them rejoicing, while in the background, the older son turned away in disgust. Dan didn't know the first thing about fifteenth century tapestries, but he knew that this was an object of exceptional beauty.

"Wow," he said.

"Well, well, well," said Mrs. Doheny, quite overwhelmed by the discovery.

"What was lost has been found," added Miss Alma.

The beauty of the tapestry seemed to add a glow to the hall. They fell silent.

"Thank you, Father," Theodore finally said ever so quietly.

Dan and Miss Alma looked up, surprised that Theodore would utter a prayer. Then they saw where he was looking. He wasn't praying at all. They hadn't noticed that over the panel behind which the tapestry had been concealed, hung a portrait of Hollis Eckert.

An Unexpected Arrest

Miss Alma decided to keep the discovery of the tapestry a secret. The first thing to be done was to take it to an art historian in Pittsburgh to make sure it was real. The woman who could do this was on vacation for a few days, so arrangements were made to drive it there on the following Monday.

Uncle Jeff arrived at the museum a few hours after the tapestry was discovered. Miss Alma took one look at him and insisted he go home and get back into bed.

"The last thing I need is the flu, Mr. March," she said.

"No offense, ma'am, but if that thing's as valuable as you think it is, even having two of us here might not be enough security." He was referring to Tony, the other security guard who had been called in to substitute for him.

Dan watched his uncle from around the corner. His hands were shaky and his skin was pale. Dan wanted to believe that his uncle hadn't been drinking, but it was tough. The truth was, it looked like he had.

Dan tried to slip out through the kitchen. He just didn't want to deal with Uncle Jeff.

Rick was on his hands and knees in the middle of the lawn measuring the grass with a ruler.

"Hey, dude. It's a sixteenth of an inch taller than it was yesterday! You *can* watch grass grow! And you know what else, dude? They're wrong. It *is* exciting!"

Dan didn't want to deal with Rick either. He didn't want to deal with anyone. He smiled, waved, and went back into the house. Miss Alma was in the kitchen. She had the envelope that Dan had left on her desk in her hand. She did not look happy.

"Is this some kind of a joke, Mr. Pruitt?" she demanded.

"No, ma'am," he answered.

She removed a paper from inside the envelope and laid it on the table. It was a photograph; a very old, beat-up photograph of President Abraham Lincoln reviewing the troops during the Civil War. In the picture, Miss Alma was standing right next to him.

"Contrary to popular belief, I was not one of President Lincoln's advisers."

"I was hoping you'd understand my point without being offended," Dan offered.

"What point is that? That I'm older than dirt? Who could possibly be offended by that?"

"No," Dan explained, "that you can't trust a photograph."

Miss Alma decided to stop being offended and listen. Dan got right to the point.

"Look, the fact is, your generation and mine have different points of view on certain things. Like with photographs. It seems to me you were ready to believe that the documents which that man brought you might have been faked, but the snapshot of him with Ethel Eckert in Paris really threw you. I wanted to prove that it shouldn't. That's why Shelby and I did this."

Dan took a deep breath. It was very important that Miss Alma understood.

"We scanned the picture of Abraham Lincoln into the computer, and then we did the same with a photo of you that was in the newspaper last month. A few adjustments, and there you are in Virginia in 1864. Look, it isn't even that good. It's the wrong kind of paper for starters, but we put it in the oven for a few minutes, did some other stuff, and made it look old. Imagine what we could have done if we'd had more time. We could have made it look as good as—"

"—as the photograph of Theodore Eckert with Ethel," said Miss Alma, finishing for him.

"Yes," said Dan.

"Any thoughts about how he knew about the tapestry? Or the secret passageway? Or so much about Hollis Eckert?" Miss Alma sounded as discouraged as Dan felt.

"No, ma'am," he answered.

"Well, I suppose I should be grateful for one thing," she added.

"What's that?" asked Dan.

"At least you didn't make up a photo of me with Adolph Hitler."

"Couldn't find a good enough picture of him," he answered.

Before he left Eckert House that afternoon, Dan had an upsetting encounter with his uncle. He walked down to the first basement to return a box of files for Miss Alma, only to find Uncle Jeff searching for something on his hands and knees.

"Dan, have you seen the keys to the security closet?" he asked.

The security closet was where, among other things, there was a safe in which the guards kept their guns. It was located on the north side of the basement beneath the Main Salon in what was once the Eckert's wine cellar.

"I know I had them ten minutes ago when I came down here on my rounds and now . . ." There was real panic in his voice.

Dan helped him look for a few minutes, but he couldn't find them either. "Uncle Jeff, it's okay. There are duplicates."

"Yeah, and Miss Alma will hand them to the guy who replaces me," he exclaimed. "I can't lose this job."

"Uncle Jeff," Dan started. He was going to ask, as delicately as he could, whether or not his uncle had been drinking. But Dan didn't finish. His eyes fell on the door to the security closet. The keys were in the lock. "Look," he said, pointing.

His uncle rushed over and pulled them out. "I promise you they weren't ..." But he didn't finish. He saw the skeptical look on Dan's face. "Thanks," he muttered. "Guess I got distracted." He left quickly.

Dan wanted to talk to his mother about Uncle Jeff, but when he got home and found that there was still no word from his father, he forgot.

"Are *you* worried, Mom?" Dan asked as he helped her get dinner on the table.

"Yes and no," was the answer. "Right here, right now, talking to you, no. But when I wake up in the middle of the night ..." She smiled. "That's when I pray for strength." She gave Dan a hug. "I always get it."

That evening, Dan took a long walk around town. Once again he found himself on East Crane Street in front of Will Stoller's house. If only Dan could talk to him. The diary ended in April of 1945, before the author revealed whether or not his father returned safely from the war. As crazy as it sounded, Dan felt that if the boy's father returned, then so would his own.

"Don't get whacko on me, Pruitt," Dan told himself. "That's superstitious, and God and superstition don't work the same side of the street."

Dan also walked by his cousin Pete's house. He told himself he wasn't spying, but he really was. He stood in the shadows and looked through the front window. Uncle Jeff was sitting on the couch with his eyes closed and a wet washcloth on his forehead. Perhaps he really did have the flu, but he could just as easily be recovering from too much alcohol.

Pete's bedroom was upstairs in the back of the house. He was practicing his trumpet. Pete wasn't the world's best trumpeter, and no amount of practice seemed to make him better. It sounded to Dan like he was trying to play "The March of the Wooden Soldiers." Then again, it was so bad it could have been "The Chicken Song." Whatever it was, it sure wasn't helping his father's headache.

But Pete was unaware of that and kept going and going and going. Hangover or flu, Dan felt sorry for his uncle, who just sat there without complaining. Dan wished he had a cell phone with him. He would have called and pretended to be one of the neighbors — and begged for mercy.

From the bushes came an ominous hiss. Dan knew it had to be Chester, Pete's very large, very aggressive cat. Chester was an animal that took naps in the road and forced cars to drive around him. It didn't matter if he saw you every day and he purred and rubbed up against you and took kitty treats from your hand. No, none of that mattered. If somewhere in the warped depths of his little cat brain (very little), you were standing or sitting or sleeping where he wanted to be, you were the enemy. At that moment, Dan was standing where Chester wanted to be. The hiss was followed by a growl. Chester was the only cat Dan had ever met that actually growled like a dog.

As Dan saw it, he had two options. He could stand his ground and fight, thus ensuring the end of his brief, but relatively happy life, or he could run like crazy. Of course running meant that Chester would follow in hot pursuit. Dan calculated that he would probably get halfway up the hill before a mighty leap from the cat would bring him to his knees.

It would be just like the lions and the zebras in those nature programs. And like the lions, Chester would sink his fangs into Dan's neck and feast on him. Running downhill was also an option, but Chester would catch him sooner, and the result would be the same.

Chester was slowly advancing. He was in that low-to-the-ground-creeping-cat posture. He wasn't going any faster than he needed to. Chester knew he had his prey right where he wanted it.

Think, man, think! Dan told himself. Then he remembered he had some change in his pocket! He took it out quietly, not making any sudden movement that would cause Chester to strike sooner.

Just next door, in the neighbor's front yard, a ceramic garden gnome stood beneath the lamppost amid the petunias. Dan hurled a quarter at the little statue and hit it with a loud PLINK. Chester, ever the hunter, whirled and sprang at the gnome without hesitation.

Dan took off up the hill as fast as he could run. He heard the neighbors' shrieks and shouts as they watched the deranged cat wrestle with — and then destroy — their beloved lawn ornament.

Dan felt a little guilty the next day when his uncle came to work with a nasty scratch on his hand. He had tried to separate the cat from the gnome.

"It was weird," Uncle Jeff explained. "After Chester mauled that elf thing — or whatever it was — he went across the street and beat up Mr. Jensen's plastic deer."

Uncle Jeff left to make his rounds and report to Miss Alma before the public was admitted. A few minutes later, Dan was coming up the long south hall from the kitchen when he heard the distinct sound of a gun being cocked. He froze. Looking into the library, he saw his uncle with his gun drawn, pointing it toward the far corner of the room.

"I know you're back there," Uncle Jeff said. "I have my gun drawn, so come out slowly."

Dan didn't make any noise. If his uncle panicked, the gun could easily be turned on him.

"I'm coming over there. I'm not kidding. I have a gun," his uncle repeated. Dan watched as his uncle disappeared around the corner of a display case. Dan held his breath. He stood still for a good three minutes, waiting for some sound of a scuffle — or worse — but nothing happened. Dan decided to risk calling out.

"Uncle Jeff? Are you okay?"

There was no answer. Dan swallowed hard and stepped into the library.

"Uncle Jeff?"

Dan rounded the corner to find his uncle leaning against the wall, sweating and trembling.

"There was someone here. I know it," Uncle Jeff muttered. "There *was*."

Dan felt sorry for him. He was really shaken up. He knew he had to say something.

"Well, it's an old house . . . lot's of strange shadows and noises . . ."

For the second time in as many days, Dan's uncle looked at him, knowing that he wasn't believed. Dan felt terrible.

"Let's tell Miss Alma we're not ready to open the museum," he suggested.

"No," Uncle Jeff said forcefully. "You're right. It was just my imagination." He replaced his gun in his holster and left.

The next day was Sunday. After church, they brought Grandpa Mike out to the backyard to sit in the shade and enjoy the mild day. Everyone was on his or her best behavior.

The Eenies had taken an interest in a board game called *Revenge!* The object was to take over a country and then drive your enemies from power. It was the perfect game for the Eenies because, as they said many times, their main goal in life was to drive Dan from the house. Dan played a couple of rounds with them and was defeated each time.

Finally, he read the sports page to Grandpa Mike. The Pirates were barely holding on to third place. Dan expressed his lack of faith in their ability to make the play-offs and tossed the newspaper aside.

As he sat there at his grandfather's feet, he felt his own discouragement growing. He was discouraged about Uncle Jeff, the events at Eckert House, and—most of all—with not hearing from his father.

A moment later, Dan was surprised to feel a hand on his head. Grandpa Mike was ruffling his hair! It was the first time he had moved his arm this much since his stroke.

"Mom!" Dan called out with excitement. Dan's mother rushed over.

"Look at you, Dad!" she said, flushed with happiness. But the excitement wasn't over. Grandpa Mike was struggling to speak.

"Ope . . . keep ope . . ." he said with great effort.

"Hope? Is that what he said?" Dan asked.

"Yes," his mother answered. "I'm sure of it."

Grandpa Mike nodded once in agreement.

"Okay, Grandpa, I won't give up."

The rest of the day was one of the happiest Dan could remember since they moved to Freemont.

But hope and happiness were in short supply the next morning. Around eleven-thirty Dan's mother got a phone call. Uncle Jeff was at a police station in Pittsburgh being questioned. The Kellenberg Tapestry was missing.

An Unexpected Clue

Dan slipped out of the house as soon as he got all the details from his mother. The only problem was, there were almost no details to be had. Uncle Jeff had driven to the museum in Pittsburgh so that the tapestry could be authenticated by the expert, but when he opened the back of the van, the tapestry was no longer there. Instead there were some old blankets rolled up inside the same kind of plastic with which the tapestry had been covered.

As Dan sped down the hill on his skateboard, he tried to believe the best of his uncle, but the fact of the matter was, he couldn't. Uncle Jeff had just been so . . . *weird* the past few days. Dan didn't like himself for thinking it, but anything was possible. About the kindest theory he could come up with was that his uncle was drunk and didn't really know what he was doing.

Dan arrived at Eckert House to find the museum closed, which made sense, considering what had happened. Dan let himself in through the back with his set of keys and found Mrs. Doheny sobbing at her small desk in the front hall.

"Oh, Daniel," she exclaimed as she rushed to him, "it's just awful. Horrible." She pulled him into a soggy embrace.

"Please, tell me what happened," he said, pulling away. He looked for a much needed tissue for her, but the only things on her desk were a screwdriver and a greasy rag. Dan thought that if Miss Alma saw those two items on the shiny surface of the antique desk, then she'd really give Mrs. Doheny something to cry about. Mrs. Doheny continued her story, but she wasn't making any sense.

"Your dear, dear uncle . . . oh, that nasty Theodore Eckert."

"What are you talking about?"

"Your uncle and Rick were loading the tapestry into the truck. That . . . that horrible man said something to my Rick about getting a haircut and looking more professional. Then Rick said something back to him about how maybe he was shabby on the outside, but at least he didn't have anything to hide on the inside—unlike some people. And then Theodore Eckert said such cruel things about my Rick. Your uncle tried to stop them both, but that Theodore went right in and demanded that Miss Alma fire my Rick. Your uncle tried to calm things down, but he couldn't. He left for Pittsburgh shortly after that. If only your uncle had stayed a little longer, I know he would have kept Miss Alma from firing my Rick."

"Miss Alma fired him?" Dan was truly shocked.

"Yes. Right there on the spot." Mrs. Doheny went on to explain that Rick did lose his temper with Miss Alma but that Theodore Eckert was worse. He even criticized Miss Alma for the way she was managing Eckert House and implied that if Miss Alma did not make some changes, then he, Theodore Eckert, would.

"But what about my uncle?" Dan was getting impatient.

Before Mrs. Doheny could answer, the doorbell rang. Neither Dan nor Mrs. Doheny moved.

"The museum is closed," she whispered. "Don't say anything. I'm sure they'll go away."

But they didn't. The bell rang again. Loud knocking followed. Tony, the security guard, came down from the second floor.

"I know you're in there!" a familiar voice cried out. It was Theodore Eckert. "I'm here with the police and a court order, so I suggest you open the door immediately."

Instinct took over. Dan sensed real danger, and as Mrs. Doheny crossed to open the front door, he slipped quietly into the library. He watched what happened next from behind a display case. Not even the security guard noticed Dan.

As Theodore Eckert stepped into the hall, he handed Mrs. Doheny some legal papers. They said that all activities at Eckert House were to stop until further notice. As soon as he made sure that Mrs. Doheny understood this, he ordered her out.

"I think we've had more than enough foolishness in this house," he snapped. Mrs. Doheny grabbed her purse and fled from the mansion. Tony was told to lock the door after her.

"You're not to let anyone into Eckert House today under any circumstances," Theodore Eckert told Tony.

"Yes, sir," Tony answered.

The policeman, Theodore, and Tony headed up to Miss Alma's office. As soon as they were gone, Dan slipped out the back door and crept off the property. He didn't want to be seen because he still had his keys to Eckert House. He knew he had to keep them.

Dan hid in the park across the street from the museum. He needed some time to figure out what to do next. He didn't know how to help his uncle, he didn't know where Miss Alma was, and Theodore Eckert was acting like he owned the museum. Dan knew it was going to be very difficult to get Theodore Eckert out. But he also knew he had to try. Dan just knew that guy was a fake. He had to be.

"Okay, go over the facts. Always go over the facts," he whispered.

Fact: Theodore Eckert had arrived in Freemont only after the statue made the news. That argued that he was in it for the money.

Fact: He had documents, pictures, and a story that —at least on the surface—added up. That argued that he was very careful to get his story as solid as possible.

Fact: Any of those things could be faked. But that's where Dan's arguments broke down, for everything that Theodore Eckert presented to Miss Alma was certainly top-notch if they were not real. Those kinds of forgeries would take time, and Theodore Eckert only had a couple of weeks to pull it all together.

"I'll come back to that one," Dan muttered.

Fact: Theodore Eckert had information about the inside of Eckert House that simply could not be faked. That argued that his story was real.

Fact: The tapestry went missing in the early 1950s, the same time that Theodore Eckert was supposed to have been in Freemont. Again, that argued that he was telling the truth.

Dan didn't like where any of this was going. All arguments were clearly on the side of Theodore Eckert's claim that he was really the son of Hollis Eckert. Dan decided that he needed Shelby and Pete. He had to be wrong. And maybe by figuring out who Theodore Eckert really was, they could somehow help Pete's dad.

As Dan stood to go, he saw a familiar figure stretched out on the green grass that surrounded Freemont's monument to its war heroes. It was Rick Doheny. Dan approached him.

"Rick, are you okay?" Dan called out as he drew near.

"What are you gonna do?" he asked, with a nod back toward Eckert House.

Rick sighed, "Time for me to move on. There are other lawns calling to me out there, dude." Rick waved an arm wide. "They need me, dude, and I'm going."

"I'm sorry," Dan offered. In truth, he kind of liked Rick. He had gotten used to his strange ways.

"Take care of my mother, dude. She's not as young as she used to be." He stopped and scratched his head. "Guess she couldn't be. And listen to your own mother, dude. Mothers are the best. I should have listened to mine yesterday when she told me to stop." Rick sighed again. He looked up at the monument and saluted as he always did when he walked by it. "Onward to glory," he said. "May all your battlefields be green." Without another word, Rick walked away.

There was something about his brief conversation with Rick that left Dan troubled, but he didn't know why. Dan leaned against the monument to look out at the river. Maybe it was because the exchange with Rick had been so short. Conversations with Rick were never short. But the more Dan thought about it, the more he kept coming back to Miss Alma and why she had been so quick to fire Rick. It just didn't make sense. Was she covering something up?

Dan turned around to look at the monument. He saluted it, too. "Our Brave and Noble Heroes" the inscription read at the top. Then there was a list of all those from the town who had died during various wars. Dan must have walked by it a hundred times without reading it.

He picked up his skateboard and started for home. After a few paces, he stopped. He ran back to the monument. There was a list of names of everyone from Freemont who had died in World War II! He eagerly scanned the list for the name of Stoller.

"Reynolds, Robinson, Santos," Dan read aloud. "Smith, Speers . . ." Dan stopped. There it was. Stoller. Henry Stoller. And the date, April of 1945, just before the war ended in Europe. "How sad," Dan whispered. He remembered that the diary ended on

April 14, 1945, the date, Dan suspected, that Will Stoller heard that his father had been killed.

"Well, God," Dan prayed, "I'm sure you took care of all these families in ways that they didn't even know at the time. But even so, it must have been a real hard thing to go through."

Dan's prayers were often like this: simple, spontaneous bursts of conversation. He realized that he didn't have these "conversations" as often as he should, so he added a silent prayer for Uncle Jeff and Pete, as well as another for his father. "There are times when I wish I knew what you knew, but I guess that would be like insider trading."

Dan was on his way out of the park, but he stopped again.

"Of course! Insider trading! That's it!" he said loud enough for people who were nearby to hear. As Dan ducked behind a tree so that no one from Eckert House could see him, he realized his "facts" had been all wrong. He also knew that he had to get back inside Eckert House right away to prove it before it was too late.

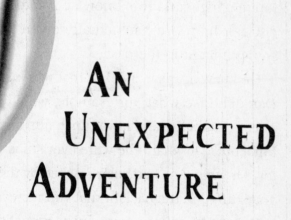

AN UNEXPECTED ADVENTURE

Dan watched from across the street as Theodore Eckert and the policeman came out of the museum. Theodore held a folder in his gloved hand. They both got into the squad car and drove away. That meant that only Tony, the security guard, was left inside. Dan crept across the street. Because he had his keys, getting into Eckert House was not going to be a problem. Getting onto the property was the challenge.

Eckert House was completely surrounded by a massive stone wall. At its lowest point, the wall was ten feet high, and Dan knew he had to scale it without any help. He had actually given this problem some thought in the past.

He knew it was weird, but that was just something Dan did. Like what, for example, would he do if his house caught fire and it was up to him to get Grandpa Mike out? Or what if he were ever stuck in an elevator? Or what if he had been grabbed by the art thieves and stuffed in the back of that van instead of Pete?

Dan wasn't exactly sure why he thought it would be necessary to sneak over the stone wall behind Eckert House, but he had given it some serious attention, and he had a plan.

There was a skinny sidewalk that ran down the hill between houses from Church Street toward the wall at the back of the Eckert House property. A scruffy hedge grew on both sides. When the sidewalk reached the wall, it took a sharp left and ran along its base all the way out to Filkins Street.

It had been many years since the sidewalk had been repaired, so it was rough and uneven. For this reason it was rarely, if ever, used by the kids of the town — at least not those on bikes, skateboards, or in-line skates. Another reason it wasn't used was the steepness of the hill and the sharpness of the turn when the sidewalk reached the wall. Anyone on wheels was going so fast at that point that the turn was almost impossible to make and a collision with the wall was a certainty. But Dan didn't plan on making the turn.

There was a large maple tree with an outstretched limb that hung over the sidewalk right near the bottom of the hill. Dan's plan involved that limb. If he made it down the hill on his skateboard without wiping out, and if he could jump off of it at just the right time, and if he could grab hold of that limb, then he had a serious shot at swinging up on the wall. A ten-foot drop to the ground on the other side would be a piece of cake compared to that.

Dan stood at the top of the sidewalk with one foot on his skateboard. He made sure no one was watching.

"Well, God," he whispered, "I don't know if this is one of those times when it's even fair for me to pray. You know why I've got to get inside, and this is the only way I can think of to do it. Please keep me safe." Dan took a deep breath, added an "amen," and pushed off.

He was surprised by how quickly he picked up speed. He had carefully examined the broken sidewalk on his way up and knew that he would have to slalom down to avoid the trouble spots. That part would be fairly easy for someone with Dan's skill, but he knew that about halfway down, a serious shift in the sidewalk that raised the concrete a good two inches would be his biggest challenge. It was coming up fast.

"Strength," he said aloud. He knew that he couldn't let his front wheels hit the bump, so his plan was to lean back and raise them off the ground just before they made contact with it. The other half of this maneuver was another split-second body shift, which would slam the front wheels back down on the pavement and force his rear wheels up in the air.

"Three, two, one," he said. BANG, he forced the front wheels up, BANG, a split second later he did the same with the back wheels. He was safely over the bump! He had no time to relax, though, for he had to veer sharply to the left to avoid a hole, then sharply to the right to avoid another. Then almost immediately, the spot where he had to make his jump was rushing toward him.

Dan looked from the sidewalk to the tree limb and back again. When he reached the spot, he ground the nose of his skateboard into the pavement, bringing it to a violent halt. Physics took over, and Dan went flying through the air. He reached out as he did and grabbed the branch of the tree! He hooked his leg over it, and before he lost his nerve, he stood up and launched himself at the wall. He landed with a thud and lay there panting for a moment.

"One of these days I'm gonna do things just a little easier," Dan grunted. "But not today." Not having a moment to spare, he swung his legs over the far side of the wall and gripped the edge with both hands. He lowered himself down, until his arms were fully extended, and dropped to the ground.

Getting to the back door was relatively easy, for he knew every shrub, bush, and tree on the property. Even someone looking out the window would have had difficulty seeing Dan as he zigzagged his way to the house. After looking through the window in the back door to make sure the kitchen was empty, Dan slipped his key into the lock and silently pushed the door open. He was safely inside.

Dan's next objective was the Main Salon. He crept up the long south hall, past the library, past the dining room, past the Little Salon, until he was at the opening of the front hall. He stopped to listen for some sound of Tony. Nothing. He stepped out into the open and froze. Tony was there, right behind Loretta. He hadn't been visible from where Dan had been standing.

Dan quickly ducked back into the shadows of the hallway. Had he been seen? He held his breath. Footsteps came closer. Dan had only one option—retreat.

As quickly and quietly as he could, Dan headed back to the kitchen. His only option once he got there was the broom closet. He ducked into it and pulled the door shut behind him.

Dan heard Tony come into the kitchen and look around, but whether he had seen Dan or was just making his rounds, Dan wasn't sure. He held very still. Tony got a drink of water and left. Hiding in the closet had an unexpected benefit. Dan was able to grab a flashlight, and considering where he was headed, it would have been foolish to go without one.

When he was sure Tony was gone, Dan emerged from the closet and crept down the hall. This time he looked into each of the rooms he passed before proceeding. When he got to the front hall, he heard Tony in the corridor above him. So he sprinted across the open space (saluting Loretta as he did, of course), and made it safely into the Main Salon.

Dan wasted no time in finding the spot on the fireplace that would open the secret door. He pressed the image of the Red Sea parting and was rewarded with a click as the secret door on the side swung open. He stepped inside, pulled the panel shut behind him, and turned on his flashlight.

Dan had good reason to return to the secret passageway. When he was inside the crawl space pulling out the tapestry, he didn't think to look around to see if there was any evidence that the space had been undisturbed for fifty years. Now he was going to find out.

He wasn't sure exactly how he was going to get *into* the crawl space, but he knew that it shared a wall with the very staircase he was climbing, and he was pretty sure that he could find a way. He remembered a strong draft when he was inside the wall, and that meant air was somehow flowing through the space.

Dan took each step very, very carefully. He could not afford to make any more mistakes. As he climbed, he went over all the mistakes he had already made.

Dan's biggest error was his assumption that Theodore Eckert had recently decided to come to Freemont. All the evidence pointed to a very careful, well-researched, and clever story that had to have taken months, if not longer, to put together: the information needed to fake the European documents, the history of the Eckert family, the "old" photographs. Theodore Eckert (or whatever his name really was) had been planning all his lies *before* Eckert House made the news. His appearance in Freemont just after all the publicity was a coincidence. What was not a coincidence, what seemed very clear, was that Theodore had help from someone right here in Eckert House, someone with inside information.

Dan wondered who it was. Who gave him all that information? The list of suspects was not a long one: Miss Alma, Rick, or Mrs. Doheny. They were the only people who had been at Eckert House long enough to know what Theodore Eckert needed to know to pull off his scam. Dan took them one at a time.

Mrs. Doheny. She had been with Eckert House since it was turned into a museum. She sat at her desk and saw everything, knew everyone. She could listen in on conversations if she chose to, and she saw every piece of mail that came in and went out. Maybe her whole ditzy weepy personality was an act.

Rick. Like Dan, Rick had keys to every door in Eckert House. Dan had found out quite a bit about the place in a very short amount of time, and Rick had had years. Rick was definitely on the weird side, but he was not stupid. Maybe he was anything but laid-back.

Miss Alma. She *was* Eckert House. There was nothing about it that she didn't know, and, truth be told, she had made it what it was. But wouldn't that get to you after a while? All the antiques and pieces of art that you could touch but not have? Maybe she brought Theodore Eckert in herself. Maybe, together, Miss Alma and Theodore Eckert were going to sell off the museum's treasures and split the take.

Dan instantly felt guilty. Mrs. Doheny? Rick? Miss Alma? They were all good, decent people. No, there had to be another solution — something he was missing.

Dan had arrived at the section of the staircase near the spot where the tapestry had been hidden. He put the flashlight down and got on his hands and knees. He didn't know what he was looking for exactly, some kind of handle or device that would open a section of the wall and allow him to get into the crawl space.

Five minutes of careful searching produced nothing. Dan checked and double-checked. After about twenty minutes, he stopped. He had been wrong. Again. If he wanted to get back into the crawl space, he would have to go out into the hall and enter it through the panel. Was it worth the risk? Was there some way to distract Tony and keep him out of the way long enough to take a good look? Dan knew he had to try, but he had no idea how he was going to do it.

"Well, that's what makes my life so exciting," he quipped. He knew the first order of business was to get Tony downstairs by creating some kind of distraction. As he headed back down the winding staircase, the beam of his flashlight caught something white hanging from a nail. Was it a piece of cloth?

Dan stopped to investigate. When he lifted the cloth up, his heart started beating faster. It was a handkerchief, a handkerchief he had seen before. There was a faint reddish-orangish stain on it, the residue of something that had been washed but did not quite come out. Tomatoes! It was Miss Alma's handkerchief! Dan couldn't believe his eyes. Miss Alma had been on this staircase. Why? He was sure Miss Alma knew about the secret staircase, but he'd never seen any sign that she ever used it.

Dan took a moment to catch his breath. Miss Alma? Was she the one behind all of this? Had she really snapped? He couldn't stand there much longer. There was too much to do. He stuffed the handkerchief into his pocket and moved swiftly and silently to the bottom of the passageway. The panel was still shut, and he felt for the three holes that triggered the spring that would open the door. He remembered the last time he had been stuck in this very spot, wondering if he would be able to get out.

Just as Dan's fingers found what he was looking for, a rough hand grabbed him from behind and covered his mouth. A sharp blow struck the back of his head. Dan fell to the ground, unconscious.

An
Unexpected
Climb

When Dan came to, he was in total darkness. His head throbbed. He raised his hand to the spot where he had been struck. He had quite a bump.

"Maybe if I take a little nap I'll feel better," he mumbled. The idea of sleep sounded good. But then something deep inside of him told him that was wrong . . . something about not falling asleep. A skateboarding accident the year before had landed him in the emergency room with a severe knock on his head. The doctor said absolutely no sleep for at least eight hours. The Eenies were given the assignment of keeping Dan awake, and they decided to do it by annoying him as much as possible. They were quite good at it.

"No sleep," Dan groaned. "Sleep is bad."

Dan wondered where he was and how he got there. He tried to think of the last thing he remembered. Speeding down the hill on his skateboard? No, he had gotten into the house, he remembered that. And he also got past the security guard and into the secret passageway. There was something about a piece of cloth or a ribbon . . . No, a handkerchief! Miss Alma's handkerchief! That's when it all came back to him, his shock at connecting Miss Alma to Theodore Eckert, the hand over his mouth and the blow to the head. There was something else, too. What?

"Think, Dan," he said aloud. He decided that talking out loud was probably a good idea. It would help him to concentrate and even stay awake.

"He picked me up and flung me over his shoulder. I remember waking up and we were going down more stairs. Then I passed out again." But just who it was that carried him, Dan could not remember. He knew that he knew—it just wasn't coming to him yet.

"Okay, now where am I?" he wondered. Dan was fairly sure that he was somewhere inside Eckert House. "But why?" he asked. "Use your brain, Pruitt."

A second later it came to him. The smell. Eckert House didn't smell bad or anything, but there was a definite scent he associated with the museum, kind of like an old, leather-bound book mixed with bits of dust. "Okay, you're in Eckert House, and you're below the main floor." His memory of being carried down and the chill in the air told him that.

Dan reached out to his left and to his right. He was in a space that was only about three feet wide. There was stone or maybe brick on one side, and planks of wood on the other. He felt over his head to see if he could stand. He could and he did.

Dan reached up as high as he could and still found no obstruction. Just as he did when he was in the crawl space pulling out the tapestry, he felt a draft of air coming from somewhere above. Next he reached out in front of him. Nothing. He slid his foot along the floor—which felt like packed dirt—and took a step. Still nothing. Another cautious step and then another. Finally, he hit a wall.

"Okay," he said, "let's try the other direction."

He proceeded with caution, eventually hitting another wall.

"So, you're in a space about three feet by seven feet, with nothing above you. The question is, how did Rick get you in here?"

Rick. That's who carried him in. Dan had come to briefly and then passed out again as Rick flung him over his shoulder. Rick had hit him on the head and hauled him down here. Rick was behind it after all. But why? Dan decided to put off answering that question until later. He realized he had a more pressing matter to deal with.

"Okay, I don't think he put me in here to die. If he wanted me dead, I think he would have killed me. Of course he could have thought I was dead already... No, he's too smart for that. He's coming back. And when he does, I'm pretty sure he's not bringing me a pizza. No, Danny Boy, you've got to get out of here."

Dan spent a good fifteen minutes looking for some sign of a door or a hole or a hatch — anything that indicated an opening. He found nothing.

"Even if you did, Rick would have blocked it from the other side. Face it, Pruitt, your only way out is up." He peered up into the darkness but saw nothing.

Dan stood against the boarded wall and reached up. A couple of feet above his head, right at the extension of his reach, there was a longish gap in the boards with enough space for him to get his fingers in. He inserted both his hands and pulled. Nothing gave way. It seemed solid, so he leaned back, braced his feet against the wall and started to climb. His back was against the solid stone wall as he moved up. The exertion made his head throb like crazy, and for a moment he thought he was going to pass out.

"This would definitely not be a good time to faint," he said, taking big gulps of air. "Stay strong, Pruitt."

The word "strong" brought him back to the Scripture his father had left him. *And Jesus grew in wisdom and stature, and in favor with God and men.*

Strength. Stature. He just wasn't measuring up these days.

"I got myself into another mess, didn't I, God? Sorry about that. Well, I'd appreciate it if you could get me out of this one, too. Not that I deserve it. But I guess it'd be cool if you could at least spare my mother the grief, if nothing else. And I promise it won't happen again. Really. I hope."

The next hour was one of the most physically and mentally exhausting of Dan's life. He would reach for some kind of fingerhold, pull himself up, rest, and reach again. In the beginning he was able to wedge himself against the two walls, his feet against the boards, his back against the stone, but about twenty-five feet up, the stone wall at his back disappeared. There was another wall there, just out of his reach — the echo of his voice told him that — but he could not touch it.

"Strength," he told himself again. "Be strong. It's what God expects of you."

The rest of the climb, wherever it led, was going to be straight up, with Dan clinging very tightly to only one wall.

Dan had no idea which part of the house he was in, but at least the boards and beams were spaced at regular intervals, so he was able to find a foothold, reach, grab a beam above, straighten, pull himself up, and rest before repeating the process.

Whenever Dan was involved in a monotonous task, he would get a song stuck in his head and repeat a certain part of it over and over again. Unfortunately, and for reasons he could not understand, that song was always "Good King Wenceslas," a Christmas carol he truly despised for its boring tune and bizarre lyrics.

Scrubbing the pots and pans: *Good King Wenceslas looked out on the feast of Stephen* ...

Shoveling the driveway: *When the snow lay round about deep and crisp and even* ...

Sweeping the garage: *Brightly shone the moon that night though the frost was cruel* ...

And each time, whatever the task, sweeping, shoveling, raking, he found himself doing it in rhythm with the song. But "Good King Wenceslas" would have been a Beethoven symphony compared to what Dan was hearing in his head as he climbed higher, for playing over and over again was the musical phrase from the diary his cousin Pete had played on his trumpet. Those six notes simply never left Dan's head. It was maddening.

"A lot of good they did us," he said, trying to get his mind to go in a different direction—any direction other than those awful six notes. "I still think it's a code of some kind. It has to be. If you want to keep information from someone, or even send it ..." Dan stopped. "Codes," he said again. "Codes." If his head wasn't hurting so much, he knew that the thought he couldn't quite pull together would come into focus.

A wave of dizziness swept over Dan. He stopped climbing and clung tightly to the wall. The possibility of his falling backwards was suddenly very real. He knew it wasn't true that the wall was tipping him back into the shaft, but the feeling was still very real.

"Stay strong," he said through gritted teeth. "God, please," he whispered as tears stung his eyes. "I need whatever you can give me now."

Be strong, a voice deep within him urged. Through sheer force of will, Dan made himself imagine the wall leaning the other way, tipping him to safety and away from danger. He told himself he was climbing a steeply pitched roof and not a vertical wall. It was just a trick, but after a minute or so, it worked. The dizziness backed off. Even so, Dan stayed motionless for a minute. A fresh draft of cool air floated down from the darkness above. Dan's breathing returned to normal.

"Think out loud," he heard himself say. "Think out loud. It'll help.

"Okay, think about what?

"You were on to something before. Go back to that.

"I was?

"You were.

"What?

"The codes.

"Oh, yeah, right. The codes.

"Well . . . ?

"Look, here's the deal. I'll do it, but on one condition.

"What's that?

"You gotta stop asking yourself questions and going back and forth like this with answers. If you don't, I'm outta here, 'cause I'm telling you right now, Pruitt, you're starting to sound a little nuts."

Dan stopped. He was surprised to find himself laughing. Then his mind went back to the idea of codes.

"Codes . . . information . . . Rick . . ."

Then it hit him. Rick must have sent Theodore Eckert information through those strange credit card charges Miss Alma had complained about. They were some kind of code. That had to be it. Dan wasn't sure how Theodore Eckert was getting copies of the bills, but he knew that somehow he was. Over a period of a few years there was no limit to the amount of information Rick could have sent from inside Eckert House.

"And another thing," Dan added, excited. "The same day that Miss Alma complained to Rick about the goofy credit card charges, she gave him her handkerchief. That means she's off the hook. Rick must have left it inside the passageway.

"Nice job, Pruitt.

"Thank you, Dan.

"Think you can break the code?

"Don't see why not.

"You don't mind that I'm talking to you like this again?

"Not really. I know that once the swelling in my head goes down I won't be crazy anymore.

"I wouldn't be so sure of that if I were you.

"What's that supposed to mean?

"Five words: *The Cuddle Bears Go Hawaiian*.

"Okay, now that's not fair. The Eenies have been watching that movie nonstop all summer.

"And isn't it funny that you seem to always find a reason to be in the room when they do.

"They're my sisters. I like spending time with them.

"Whatever. By the way, where'd you get the cut on your hand?

"What cut?"

Dan looked closely at his right hand. It was bleeding.

"I have no idea, maybe I—" Dan stopped. He could see his hand! Light was coming in from somewhere!

Dan tightened his grip and slowly looked up. The very act of tilting his head brought back the dizziness, and he had to shut his eyes. When his head stopped swimming, he opened them again. There was some kind of opening maybe six or seven feet above him. A weak gray light shone through. It was nighttime.

The last six feet should have been easy. The beams he used to haul himself up were wider and easier to stand on, but Dan was so exhausted that he wasn't sure he could do it.

Go, came a voice from deep inside of him again. *You're running out of time. You can do it.* With every ounce of strength he had left, Dan pulled himself up to the opening and looked out.

From the view, Dan realized he was almost to the roof of the South Wing. He had climbed up three full stories, plus however many feet below the ground he was when he started. The opening was covered with fancy scrolled iron and a mesh screen. It was part of the original house, and Dan guessed that it was probably used for ventilation.

"Now what?" Dan wondered. He had no idea what time it was or if anyone was around. Chances were Rick Doheny was still in the house. If Dan yelled to attract attention, Rick would know that Dan was trying to escape. To make matters worse, Dan was at the back of the house. In fact he could see the spot on the wall he had scaled to get in earlier that day. The chances that anyone in Freemont would hear him from where he was were remote.

A second later, all of that became unimportant, for Dan heard a sound from down below. A scuffling sound mixed with heavy breathing. Dan held his breath and listened. Someone else was in the wall! Someone was climbing up after him!

"Hello?" Dan called out cautiously.

"How ya' doing, dude?" a familiar voice called out. "I gotta give you points for brainpower. Those little gray cells of yours have been doing their job." He continued to climb, and it sounded to Dan like he was coming up fast. "I've been listening to you for quite some time now. You got most of it just about right, Dude."

Rick's voice was anything but laid-back and happy. He was only about a story or so below Dan, and he was angry.

"I'm not a praying man myself, dude, but you might want to start talking to the Big Guy again. You see, one of us is not coming out of here alive."

AN
UNEXPECTED
ESCAPE

Dan knew Rick could move up toward the top of the shaft faster than Dan had. For one thing he was stronger. For another, he wasn't suffering from a head injury.

"Go away, Rick. I won't say a word of this to anyone," Dan yelled.

"People always say that, dude, and then people always change their minds."

"I'm not like other people."

"True enough, dude. We're all unique creature. no two of us alike. Just like blades of grass."

Dan figured he had four minutes at the most before Rick would reach him. He had to do something, but what? He had nothing to fight Rick with, nothing but the clothes he was wearing. *My clothes,* Dan said to himself. *Well, it's a start.*

Dizzy or not, he had no choice but to move quickly. Dan lifted his foot and, holding very tightly with one hand, pulled his shoe off with the other. Now he had to figure out exactly where Rick was.

"Who is Theodore Eckert?" Dan asked. He wanted to know of course, but more importantly he had to get Rick's position.

"Just some dude I met a few years ago," came the answer. It sounded like Rick was climbing up the middle, just as Dan had.

"So Hollis Eckert isn't his father?"

"Who's to say?" Rick said. "Can any of us really be sure of who we are?"

Dan threw the shoe as hard as he could. A yell from Rick told him he'd hit his target.

"That wasn't very nice, dude," Rick said through gritted teeth.

"Oh, and killing me is? Dan shouted back.

"That was your choice. You didn't have to go snooping around."

Dan took his other shoe off and threw it.

"You missed, dude." Rick laughed. "I was waiting for the other shoe to drop."

Dan looked back out the window.

"Help!" he yelled.

"No one's out there," Rick called up. "It's almost midnight."

But Rick was wrong. Someone was out there. On the other side of the wall, at the spot where Dan had launched himself off his skateboard, he saw what looked like flashlight beams shining up into the tree. Of course! Dan had been missing for hours, and they were out looking for him. Unless someone had come along and taken it, his skateboard was exactly where he left it.

"Help!" he called again. "I'm up here under the roof on the South Wing! Help! Pete! Shelby! Mom!"

Rick only laughed. It was clear to Dan that unless someone in the search party heard him, Rick would get to him first.

He yelled louder. "Help! It's me, Dan Pruitt! I'm up here! Rick Doheny is trying to kill me!"

Suddenly there was a figure standing on top of the wall. Whoever it was had a flashlight in his hand and was shining it down into the grounds of Eckert House. There was an urgency to the motion, and it seemed to Dan that they must have heard him.

"I'm up here! Hurry! Up here just under the roof! Rick is trying to kill me!" Dan turned back to Rick. "They're out there. They know."

"Nice try, but I'm not buying it."

With every ounce of strength in his body, Dan held on to the wall with one hand and took his belt off with the other. It was the only thing he could think of to use as a weapon.

"Help! I'm up here!" he yelled again. Once again, dizziness took hold of him. *You will not give in to it,* he told himself. *You will stay strong.*

Something brushed his foot. It was Rick's hand. Dan jerked his foot away.

"Hello, dude," Rick said evenly.

With all of his might, Dan whip-snapped the belt, buckle first, toward the shadow that was Rick's head. He connected. Rick let out a howl. Dan struck again. Again Rick screamed in pain. The third time he struck, Dan missed completely. Rick had backed down a few feet.

"Help!" Dan called out once more.

Very faintly, from down below, Dan heard his name called.

"Dan Pruitt? Dan?"

"Yes, it's me! I'm up here! Please hurry! Rick Doheny's after me!"

Rick heard the voices too.

"Well, what do you know? The cavalry to the rescue. Think they'll get here in time?"

With that, Rick made another lunge for Dan. Dan was ready for him. The belt snaked out in the darkness and caught him again. Then again. And again. Dan made sure never to strike him from the same direction twice. Rick let out a yell, and then Dan heard a thud. Rick had fallen. But whether through brute strength or dumb luck, he'd somehow stopped his fall after several feet. He was breathing hard, though, and clearly injured.

"You know what?" Rick said. "You're not worth dying for. There are ways out of here that even Miss Alma doesn't know about. They'll never find me."

The sounds of Rick moving back down into the darkness came up to Dan, but something was wrong. The dizziness was back, and he knew there was no fighting it this time. He was afraid that he was going to plunge down into the darkness.

"Not now... not after all this," he whispered hoarsely. With all the strength he had left, Dan threaded the belt through the iron grill and then secured it around his waist. His last memory was of flashlight beams hitting the opening from below. He realized even then that they might not get to him in time, but he knew he'd done everything he could to survive. Now strapped to safety, Dan surrendered to the blackness.

Dan awoke to a dazzling white light.

"He's awake!" shouted a familiar voice.

"He opened his eyes! He did!"

The Eenies were nearby. Dan tried to turn his head to see them, but it hurt too much. He closed his eyes again. The light was too bright.

"If you go back to sleep, we'll ... we'll ..." For once the Eenies couldn't finish a sentence. Dan heard muffled sniffles as someone led them away.

"It's all right, ladies, he's over the worst of it now," said a soothing voice.

"Dan? Dan, can you hear me?" This time it was his mother speaking.

"Yes," he whispered.

"You're in the hospital. You have a severe concussion, but the doctor says you're going to be fine. Do you understand?"

Dan understood, but there was something important he had to ask. If only his head would stop aching. If only he could focus.

"Rick . . . it was Rick Doheny," He whispered. "Did you catch him?"

No one answered. Dan opened his eyes again. This was important. He had to push through the pain. There were several people in the room: his mother, Miss Alma, Pete, a nurse, and a man in a suit. Miss Alma, Dan's mother, and the man in the suit were all talking in whispers.

"Not polite to keep secrets," Dan finally said.

"The boy's right," Miss Alma declared. "He has as much right to know as anybody. Maybe more."

Dan's mother crossed back to him. "He got away, Dan. But the FBI is sure they'll catch him."

"FBI?"

"Yes. Technically, you were kidnapped." She told him that the man in the suit was Agent Havens from the FBI. "We'll explain it all to you later."

"What day is it?" Dan asked.

"Wednesday," his mother answered.

Wednesday? All this had happened on Monday. Didn't they think he'd rested enough? Even as he thought this, though, Dan felt very drowsy. Still, he had one more question. "Uncle Jeff?"

"I'm right next to you," he heard a familiar voice say. Dan turned to see his uncle in the next hospital bed. He was hooked up to an IV

"If we admit one more family member, we get a group rate," he joked.

Dan smiled and fell asleep.

Dan woke up in the middle of the night to find his uncle sitting in the chair next to him. He said he was more comfortable sitting up, but Dan knew that was just a cover. He knew how worried his uncle was about him.

"Uncle Jeff, why are you here?" Dan finally asked.

"Pneumonia," he answered. He seemed almost happy about it. He explained that he thought he just had the flu and that he took a bunch of over-the-counter medicine to keep going. He knew he should have gone to the doctor, but he was so concerned about Theodore Eckert's presence that he wanted to be at the museum as much as possible.

"So all that time you were just sick," Dan said,

feeling very guilty. "I thought . . . ." But Dan couldn't finish.

"I would have thought the same thing about me if I were you," Uncle Jeff said. "And for the record, you have my permission to ask me if I've been drinking any time you want. I promise I won't be offended."

Dan looked at his uncle. He meant what he said.

Uncle Jeff continued, "By the way, we don't know everything Rick and Theodore Eckert did, but Miss Alma is pretty sure they were trying to throw me off balance with stuff like taking my keys and making me think people were in the room when they weren't, and all those other strange things that happened. Apparently there are secret passageways and doors all over that house. Anyway, the idea was to get me so confused that when I got to Pittsburgh without the tapestry, I'd look like some kind of nut—which I did. Of course being sick helped."

Dan asked his uncle to fill him in on what happened when he was arrested.

"We still don't know how they did it, but when I got to Pittsburgh with the van, the tapestry was gone. The security people at their museum thought I was acting a little strange, so they kept me around without telling me why. I was pretty spaced out at that point. My temperature was something like 105. I remember telling them that I had tickets to *The Cuddle Bears on Ice* and if I didn't leave right then I was going to miss the kickoff."

"Oh, great." Dan laughed.

"Yeah, and I got into an argument with them about whether or not penguins could be trained to play water polo."

Uncle Jeff explained that Theodore Eckert was the one who demanded the authorities in Pittsburgh detain him.

"I never actually went to jail," he explained, "because one of the policemen realized how sick I was and rushed me to the hospital. Of course I had an officer at my door at all times, but that was better than being behind bars." Then Uncle Jeff explained how Theodore Eckert went to a judge and got him to shut Eckert House down.

Dan told his uncle how he had hidden and saw Theodore Eckert arrive with the papers. As he was finishing, Dan suddenly realized how the tapestry might have been switched.

"Uncle Jeff, tell me what happened at Eckert House that morning."

Uncle Jeff gave Dan the same story about Theodore

Eckert picking a fight with Rick that Dan had heard from both Rick and his mother.

"Mrs. Doheny was there when you were loading the van, right?"

"Yeah, she was."

"She didn't go into the house with you, did she?"

Uncle Jeff thought for a moment. "No, she didn't."

"Was she still there when you came out?"

"Yeah, and I was real confused because she handed me a set of keys and said I'd dropped them. I thought I was going a little crazy."

"That was part of their plan," Dan stated.

"How did you know about Mrs. Doheny?" Uncle Jeff asked.

"I saw a greasy rag and a screwdriver on her desk just before Theodore Eckert and the policeman came in. It didn't occur to me until now what it meant."

"You want to tell me?"

Dan explained his theory. He believed that first Mrs. Doheny switched the license plates on the two identical vans, and then moved the vans. The tapestry never even left Freemont.

"So Mrs. Doheny was part of it?"

Dan realized what he had just said. Mrs. Doheny was also guilty! "Has she disappeared, too?" he asked.

Uncle Jeff didn't think so, but he excused himself to make a call to the police. Before he got back, Dan fell asleep again.

Dan was allowed visitors the next day. Bit by bit, with information from Shelby and Pete, from Miss Alma, and from Agent Havens, he pieced together what happened.

The vans were checked, and Dan was correct. The license plates had been switched. Mrs. Doheny had locked herself in her own bedroom. When they found her, she confessed to everything. She explained that she did it because Rick had threatened her.

As far as anyone could tell, switching the vans was her only involvement in the entire incident. Dan felt sorry for her. Unlike everyone else who simply thought Rick was an odd duck, Dan had seen his dangerous side firsthand and knew he was capable of violence. At Miss Alma's insistence, no charges were filed against Mrs. Doheny.

When Dan told Miss Alma what he suspected about the code on the credit card bills, she went to Eckert House and brought back copies of them for Pete and Shelby. The code, as it turned out, was actually quite simple. Shelby broke it in a matter of minutes. Each number stood for a letter.

"For example," she said as she laid out her sheets of paper, "these charges of $12.56 and $20.16 and $114.50 and $12.00 spell out 'left panel,' which is where the tapestry was found, right? There are some irregularities, like sometimes zero is a placeholder, and sometimes he didn't bother, but for the most part, that's the way he did it."

Pete nodded. "He used the whole surfer-dude personality as a cover. Miss Alma just thought he was weird."

"Which he was," Miss Alma insisted. It was Miss Alma's belief that part of the thrill for Rick was doing all of this right in front of everyone without them knowing it.

Agent Havens agreed with her. In his opinion, Rick was the kind of criminal who enjoyed feeling he was smarter than everyone. "This was just a game, a way for him to thumb his nose at the world."

"But the code seems like an awful lot of trouble," Dan said. "Why didn't he just make some calls from a phone booth and set it up that way? It's not like anyone would have been able to trace them."

"You're right. The fact is," Agent Havens said, "Rick could have given his partner the information any number of ways. The credit card code was a way for him to prove how clever he was, to say, 'I dare you to figure this out and stop me.' Fortunately, you did."

Later, when Shelby spent even more time with the numbers, she saw how Rick had told Theodore all about the hidden passageway and other secrets in the house. As for how Theodore Eckert got the bills, Agent Havens explained that.

"A few phone calls gave Theodore all the information he needed. Legally his name *is* Theodore Eckert, and the credit card is issued to the Eckert Foundation. It didn't take much to convince someone in Accounting to send him a duplicate copy of the bill each month. Rick Doheny was communicating freely with him, and no one ever knew it. They never had to meet or even speak on the phone."

Something Agent Havens said confused Dan. "That old man really is Theodore Eckert?"

"In name only," replied Miss Alma. "I could change my name to Snow White if I wanted to, but it wouldn't make me any more beautiful."

"Or nicer," added Dan. He smiled, hoping Miss Alma would get the joke. She did. She let out a kind of snort which, for Miss Alma, passed as a laugh.

"Actually I have you and Shelby to thank for helping me catch him in his lies," she said. "It all started with that charming picture of me inspecting the troops with Abraham Lincoln. You made a comment that afternoon, something about my generation and modern technology. So I started thinking more twenty-first century than nineteenth."

What Miss Alma had tried to do was get Theodore Eckert's fingerprints. The hope was to take them to the police and have them run a criminal check. However, the man never removed his gloves, so that proved a dead end.

"Then he personally handed me the evidence that convicted him. You were there, Mr. Pruitt. He pulled that envelope out from behind the fireplace and said that Hollis Eckert had sealed it and placed it there in 1951."

"DNA!" shouted Pete.

Miss Alma nodded. "Exactly."

Dan didn't know a lot about DNA, but he did know that in the blood, cells, and even saliva of every human, there were specific molecules that were unique to each person. Just like fingerprints, no two people's DNA was alike. But family members had certain DNA molecules in common.

Miss Alma had taken the envelope supposedly licked by Hollis Eckert, and another sealed by her friend Ethel Eckert from many years ago (they had written each other regularly) to a crime lab. There was enough DNA on both for identification. It was determined that the person who sealed Theodore Eckert's envelope could not possibly be related to Ethel Eckert.

"And since Hollis was Ethel's uncle, that proved Theodore Eckert was lying." Beyond that, she explained, a sample from Theodore Eckert himself, taken once he was arrested, showed that he had sealed the envelope himself.

Agent Havens explained that Theodore Eckert's fingerprints matched those of a Belgian criminal named René Bouvon who escaped from a prison in Brussels some fifteen years ago.

So that was it. The mystery was solved. All the pieces came together.

"But the bad guy got away," said Dan. "And the tapestry is still missing."

"But the good guy got away, too," Dan's mother said, hugging him.

"And people are more important than things," added Miss Alma.

An
Unexpected
Friend

Dan grew stronger each day, and by
Saturday morning he was allowed to go
home. The short trip wore him out,
and he had to lie down when he got
there. When he woke up, there was a
letter from his father propped up on
his nightstand. Dan tore it open.
Noting the date, he realized it had
taken more than two weeks to get to
the States.

The letter wasn't very long. When Dan's father was flying, there simply wasn't time to write a lot. One part in particular stood out. Dan read it over and over again.

In my last letter you might remember that I said it's what a man does when no one's looking that really tells him who he is. The thing is, though, Danny, you're never really alone. God is always right beside you, and I want you to know that I'm praying that you'll feel his strength and power whenever you need it. Don't forget to ask for his help. You'll be amazed by the results.

Dan thought of the voice that urged him on as he was making the long climb. As he thought back on the experience, he realized he never really did feel alone. That feeling gave him strength. "Thanks again," he whispered.

Dan spent some time with Grandpa Mike before dinner. He tried to read from the sports page, but found he couldn't concentrate.

"Sorry, Grandpa, it's just too hard," Dan said as he lowered the paper and rubbed his head.

Grandpa Mike slowly raised his hand and patted Dan on the arm. That simple motion made everything all right. Grandpa Mike was getting stronger.

The touch of his grandfather's hand triggered something else in Dan, deep feelings that he had been keeping stuffed down inside, feelings of fear and anger and loss and relief. They were all suddenly released at once, and Dan allowed himself to really cry for the first time. Grandpa Mike didn't seem to mind at all. In fact, it felt like he understood.

After dinner, the doorbell rang and the Eenies raced to answer it.

"Surprise!" they yelled.

It was Shelby and Pete. But there was someone else with them as well.

"Dan Pruitt, this is Mr. Will Stoller. Mr. Stoller, this is my cousin, Dan," said Pete.

Will Stoller walked over to Dan.

"So this is the young man who likes to stare at my house at night," Mr. Stoller said. He shook Dan's hand. He seemed friendly enough, not at all the bitter shut-in that Dan had imagined.

Pete and Shelby explained that the Eenies had been so upset when Dan was hurt that they wanted to do something for him.

"They'd heard us talking about Mr. Stoller and the diary and decided that they would get him to talk."

"We kept going over there and bugging him until he answered the door!"

"We were very good at it."

"Indeed," Mr. Stoller added. He did not seem upset. "I'm sorry to tell you that the diary isn't mine."

Dan was disappointed, there was no question about it, but considering the events of the past week, it was a disappointment he could live with. There was an answer to that particular mystery, and he was sure they'd find it.

"Oh," was all he could say. Then he remembered the name of Henry Stoller chiseled into the monument in the park. It was the discovery of that name, and Dan's reaction to the thought of God's overwhelming knowledge, that had led him to start putting together the pieces of the mystery. In a very real way, the diary led him to figure out that Theodore Eckert was working with someone on the inside. He asked Mr. Stoller if Henry Stoller was his father.

"My oldest brother."

"I'm sorry," Dan said with all sincerity.

"Thank you." Mr. Stoller cleared his throat. He obviously had more to say. They waited. "I should tell you, my father fought in the war for Germany. It was our great embarrassment. He left us shortly after I was born to join Hitler's gang of thugs. Because of that, my mother taught us to keep to ourselves. I'm afraid it's a lesson I took to heart. And when you believe that people are thinking the worst of you, well . . ." He gave them a weak smile. "But even an old man can change."

Dan remembered how he'd thought the worst of Uncle Jeff, and even of Hollis Eckert. Maybe, just maybe, if he hadn't jumped to the wrong conclusions, things would not have gotten so out of hand.

Mr. Stoller continued. "I read some of the diary, and I do know how that young boy felt. I went through many of the same things he did while waiting for news of my brother. If you ever need to talk, Mr. Pruitt, I'd be more than happy to listen."

"Thank you, Mr. Stoller, I'd like that."

Pete took the diary and thumbed through it.

"Mr. Stoller, does the boy who wrote the diary sound like anyone you knew? Is there anything in here that might help us figure out who he is?"

Mr. Stoller gave Pete's question serious thought. "I'll tell you what," he finally said. "Why don't you bring it over to my house when Mr. Pruitt is feeling better, and we'll go through it page by page."

They all agreed that sounded like a good plan. Mr. Stoller stood to leave.

"And if you want to bring that fine-looking woman with you, by all means, feel free. Just don't tell her I told you to do it."

They were confused.

"What woman?" Dan asked.

"Miss Alma Louise Stockton LeMay, of course," he answered. "I've had my eye on her for, oh, going on thirty years now. She's the one that got away." He waved and walked out the front door.

They were all too stunned to say anything. Finally Dan broke the silence. "I think Miss Alma and I have a few things to talk about."

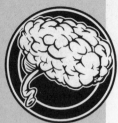

Smarter

What is **2:52** ?

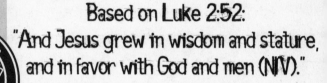

Based on Luke 2:52:
"And Jesus grew in wisdom and stature,
and in favor with God and men (NIV)."

2:52 is designed just for boys 8-12!
This verse is one of the only verses in
the Bible that provides a glimpse of Jesus
as a young boy. Who doesn't wonder
what Jesus was like as a kid?

Become smarter, stronger, deeper,
and cooler as you develop
into a young man of God
with 2:52 Soul Gear™!

Stronger

Deeper

Smarter = "Wisdom" = mental/emotional
Stronger = "Stature" = physical
Deeper = "Favor with God" = spiritual
Cooler = "Favor with men" = social

*For a Complete listing of 2:52 products
visit www.zonderkidz.com*

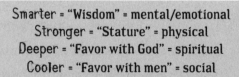

Cooler

2:52 Mysteries of Eckert House

Three friends seek to uncover the hidden mysteries of Eckert House in this four-book series is filled with adventure, mystery, and intrigue.

2:52 Mysteries of Eckert House: Hidden in Plain Sight [Book 1]

Written by Chris Auer
Eerie stories surround the old Victorian mansion-turned-museum known as Eckert House. But what was once thought to be fiction may prove to be fact after twelve-year-old Dan Pruitt makes a gruesome discovery.
Softcover 0-310-70870-2

2:52 Mysteries of Eckert House: The Chinese Puzzle Box [Book 3]

Written by Chris Auer
Dan and his friends discover a riddle hidden in an ancient Chinese puzzle box, but someone is trying to get them out of Eckert House. Whoever it is will stop at nothing to get rid of them!
Softcover 0-310-70872-9

2:52 Mysteries of Eckert House: The Forgotten Room [Book 4]

Written by Chris Auer
Dan Pruitt's certain he's found a hidden room. But when he and his friends set out to find it, they uncover more than a room. What they find will ultimately lead to danger; how will they keep their secret safe and protect themselves too?
Softcover 0-310-70873-7

Available now at your local bookstore!

Zonderkidz.

We want to hear from you. Please send your comments about this book to us in care of zreview@zondervan.com. Thank you.

Zonder**kidz**.

Grand Rapids, MI 49530
www.zonderkidz.com